Reconsider

M. J. Padgett

MJ Padgett Books LLC

Contents

Chapter One

Gracie

WHOEVER THOUGHT LEAVING AN entire classroom full of second graders unattended in a library was a good idea should come and shelve the 234 books they left strewn about the reading room. I pick up yet another jelly-smeared book and wipe down the plastic cover before putting it in its correct place. It's tedious, but such is the life of a librarian.

"Who gave them glue? Why would anyone give seven-year-olds glue in a library?" Shelby asks as she peels several pages apart.

"Are you sure it's glue?" I ask. "I didn't give them any—"

"Oh! Oh, gross!" she whines. "It's boogers." Shelby gags and runs for the bathroom while I eye the book. It looks like trash to me, so I grab it by the corner and toss it, noting I'll have to budget for new copies of several books the kids destroyed.

I sigh and gather up the next pile.

"Gracie!" Shelby screams from the bathroom. This cannot be good. Hesitantly, I head to the hallway to see what sort of disaster the children caused. The second I set foot on the carpet, I know it's bad. It's so, so bad. The carpet is soaked, and my heels squish with each step until I reach the flooded bathroom.

"Oh. My. Goodness." My jaw falls open as I take in the disaster. The toilet is like a geyser because, somehow, a child managed to burst a pipe behind it. And that does not even begin to complete the list of things wrong. There are no less than six paperback books stuffed in the bowl, along with gobs of toilet paper. Someone used a red marker to write *Mrs. Harmon is a doodie head* across the wall. And don't get me started on the stash of feminine products stuck to the opposite wall.

"Can I quit?" Shelby asks.

"Not unless you want me to hate you forever." I sigh and brave the rushing geyser to turn off the water behind the toilet. Once the spout stops spraying everything and I'm soaked, I sigh again. "I'll get a mop."

"Get a bulldozer and tear it all down." Shelby is annoyed, but it's a public library. I can't exactly ban the public from entering and using the facilities. However, I agreed wholeheartedly with whoever called Mrs. Harmon a doodie head. It would have been nice if she had minded her students rather than texting all afternoon, but there's not a lot I can do about it.

I tie my hair up and prepare to spend most of the evening cleaning the mess. It's not fair to leave it all for the janitorial crew, and besides, I have no desire to head home and face the quiet again. My nightly talks with my best friend have been nonexistent lately. Since childhood, Nina and I have shared everything, so I thought it was only natural that I tell her I swapped spit with her brother in the parking lot of a feed store. I had not anticipated her reaction to be anger, but if I'm honest, I should have expected it. After all, Paul has been my nemesis for years.

My lips curl in annoyance just thinking about him. But that kiss... My heart speeds up, so I shake my head and refocus on the monumental task ahead of me.

"No! No, get out! Out!" Shelby's screams startle me, so I rush back to the main room only to be accosted by the duck that lives in the pond out front. He's flapping around and honking, but I don't blame the poor thing. It's difficult to see where the pond ends and the library entrance begins.

"What happened?" I scream.

"The front door was left wide open, and he flew in!" She's chasing it out with a broom, but every time it reaches the door, it slips around her and runs back into the main library again. This has gone from a mess to an epic disaster, and honestly, I can't take it anymore. I've got a pregnant mare at home that needs my attention, a leaky roof, an empty cupboard, and three bald tires. I do not get paid enough for any of this, and with my best friend mad at me, I've had it up to my eyeballs.

I stare at the duck running in a circle around the World War II exhibit, Shelby swatting at it with a broom while screaming obscenities, and I wonder if this is it. Is this what it will be like for the rest of my life? Scraping and saving only to lose it all when the next disaster strikes? And oh, do they strike. Every month, it's something else. My house is two major repairs away from condemnation, I'm sure, and all I want to do is sell everything and live in the forest with my horses far, far away from civilization... and Paul Loughton.

Who walks through the front door like nothing insane is happening, and it's all just another Wednesday at the local library. Despite his boots sloshing on the carpet, the sounds of Shelby screaming, and my death-inducing glare, he strides up to me and scowls.

"Would you *please* stop sending rescue farm animals to my brother's house? Ten sheep? Really, Gracie? Don't you think the chickens, a donkey, and goats were enough? Now you send sheep and a *pig?*"

I deepen my glare. Okay, fair enough, I brought this on myself, but can he not see the destruction happening all around him?

"May is the sweetest, but she can't supervise the building of a salon and take care of a hundred animals, Gracie. John ripped into me like a rabid beast this morning, and if you don't stop, he'll end up... sending them... *what* is going on here?" he asks as he scans the library for the first time since he waltzed in with his high and mighty attitude. He blinks, and his gaze sweeps back to me.

"I'm a little busy."

Shelby manages to get the front door closed with the duck on the opposite side. She blows strands of loose hair from her face and leans against the wall. "I love you, but if you ever let another classroom of kids in here again, I really will quit." Her gaze lands on Paul and she stands straight again. "Oh, hi. When did you get here?"

Gross. She's making googly eyes at my nemesis, which makes my stomach churn. Okay, so he's hot. Paul has dark blonde hair and green eyes, unlike his brothers. However, *like* his brothers, he's muscular in all the right places, and I'm trying to ignore that fact as he stares down at me, expecting something more in reply. The jerk has the nerve to be swoony after everything he did to me in middle and high school, and I'm supposed to just stand here and take it? No, sir, I will not.

"Shelby, this is Paul. Paul, Shelby, my assistant. Now, excuse me. I have a lot of cleaning to do." I maneuver around him, but he's on my heels.

"Why is there water everywhere?" he asks.

"Kids flooded the bathroom. Broken pipe," Shelby says, her eyes glued to him. She's heard a million stories about him, but this is the first time she's seen him in person. I get it. He's nice to look at, but I wish she would stop staring at him.

Paul arches an eyebrow, which I can't help noticing since I can't seem to drag my gaze from his stupid face. I narrow my eyes and start mopping the linoleum-covered kids' area. The books are a total loss at this point since they are sitting in a puddle of water an inch deep. Paul sidles over to the World War II display and browses the books. He rearranges them while biting his lip.

"The Doolittle Raid occurred *after* the bombing of Pearl Harbor." His indignation rubs me the wrong way. It isn't as if I haven't fixed that display a hundred times already, but I can't help it if people don't put things back where they belong.

"I know. Is there anything else you need, Paul?"

He drags his frowny face away from the display long enough to shoot me a glare. "No, just stop sending animals to John's house." He steps closer and points at me. "And don't even *think* about sending them to Edwin instead. I know you. If I'm not completely clear about what I mean, you'll find a way to wiggle around it and continue torturing me."

"I wouldn't send farm animals to Edwin's apartment. I'm not crazy," I say. Shudder the thought. Edwin would probably scowl me to death.

"Or anyone else. No more farm animals, Gracie. I mean it. I don't know what I ever did to you, but John and Edwin are not me. Messing with them right now is mean. You know they're both planning weddings."

Boy, don't I know. It was all Nina talked about when she wasn't fussing at me for kissing Paul.

"Yeah. Okay, fine, but I really need to get this cleaned up and pray I don't get fired."

Paul looks around again and shakes his head, then exits the way he came. Shelby watches him go, probably trying to figure out how to chase him down without seeming desperate. It only makes the anxiety broil deeper into my chest and stomach. That stupid kiss. Why did I even do that?

One minute, we were arguing, really going at each other with the usual name-calling and threats, and the next, I just... kissed him. That alone was freaky enough, but he kissed me back. I can't stop thinking about why he did it, and I don't have the guts to ask him, so I suffer in my confusion instead of being an adult.

"Did you really send farm animals to his house?" Shelby asks, tossing books into the trash.

"His brother's house. I can't stand him."

"His brother?" She tilts her head in confusion.

"No, I adore his brothers. I dislike him."

"Why?" She pauses to assess my statement and arches an impeccably manicured eyebrow. "You say that, but the tone indicates otherwise. Still, tell me why you *think* you hate him."

I shoot her a glare as I wring out the mop and go for another swipe. "It's a long story."

Shelby chuckles and motions around the building. "I think we have time. Tell me the story while we clean. It might make the time pass faster."

I let my mind wander back over the years, but one day sticks out as the day things went from bad to worse. Sixth grade. My twelfth birthday party. All I wanted in the whole world was Paul Laughton's attention. In fairness, I got it. In fact, I got *all* of his attention and then some when he and all of his hooligan friends rampaged through the backyard like a band of crazy monkeys. In the process, he bumped into me, and I lost my balance. With my arms flailing like a baby bird, I landed in the pool, but only *after* flashing everyone in school my undies as my dress flew up. Paul pointed and laughed like a fat piglet. He helped me out of the pool, but by then, the damage was done. I was known as *that girl Gracie with the polka-dotted underpants* until high school graduation.

I relay this to Shelby, who can't stop laughing.

"Is that really a reason to hate him?"

I stomp my foot. "He apologized, but he didn't mean it, Shells. He's such a jerk." I failed to mention the *moment* we had later in my kitchen. After everyone had gone and I was finally dry, he'd come to apologize. I'd been rummaging for ice cream when he approached me from behind. When I turned around, he was so in my space there wasn't a breath between us. Staring commenced. He leaned down a fraction, his eyes focused on my lips... then he cleared his throat, said, "My mom said I had to apologize. I'm sorry," and he left.

"Did I mention he also read my diary in seventh grade and told my crush that I was obsessed with him?" And... when he found me crying under the bleachers that afternoon, he sat beside me and shared his leftover lunch snacks. He apologized—genuinely this time—and brushed my hair behind my ear. He told me I deserved better than that guy anyway, and then he left and didn't speak to me for three weeks.

I sigh. "I got teased even more for that."

Shelby bites her lip to keep from laughing harder.

"Oh, shut up before I throw booger books at you. That's not all he did. He practically tortured me for years, and you're supposed to be my friend. You should be on my side no matter what!"

Shelby throws her head back and laughs at my expense, so I rummage the booger book from the trash and throw it at her. She dodges it with a squeal.

"I warned you! Paul Loughton is the world's biggest jerk. He never apologizes for anything he does wrong, and if he does, he doesn't mean it. The whole farm animal thing is just one more stunt in a years-long feud."

"A feud? You know who else had a feud?"

I gag. "Gross. This is *not* a Shakespearean tragedy. Incidentally, if he poisoned himself, I'd be okay with it." I shrug, but regret instantly tugs at my heart. It's not true. I don't like him, but I don't really hate him. I don't know how I feel, but thinking about him dropping dead doesn't sit well with me.

"Whatever you say, Gracie. Seems to me like all of that teasing might mean a little more. What do they say about boys who tease girls?"

I lean on my mop handle and glare at her. "I will throw more books at you."

She chuckles and gets back to her work while I ponder her words. If the pool incident and the diary weren't enough reasons to avoid him back then, the almost kiss at prom definitely is. I purposely don't tell Shelby about that either. Only Nina knows, and she swore long ago to keep it a secret until the day she dies.

I got stood up at prom. I looked like an absolute dork standing in a darkened corner all by myself while everyone else had a great time, including Paul, who had attended alone. Despite our feud, I accepted when he asked me to dance. There was something about the dim lights, the soft music, the way he held me and stared down at me... it felt nice. For a second, I forgot who he was and laid my head on his shoulder. Paul stopped swaying and froze, so I looked back up at him. Centimeter by centimeter, we grew closer. A hairsbreadth away from kissing, the music changed, and Paul leaped away from me like I had leprosy.

We never spoke of it again, and he went right back to pulling pranks on me the next day. I ended the school year with purple hair, thanks to him. I have the graduation picture to prove it.

Shelby and I finish cleaning the library in silence, both of us in a rhythm that gets us through the misery quickly. After locking up, I fall into my beat-up car and head home to an empty, run-down house that's quickly sucking away my will to live.

And all I can think about the whole way home is that first almost-kiss at prom. The real kiss we shared at the feed store and how confused I am about everything in my life.

Chapter Two
Paul

MAY AND CALLIOPE STARE back at me as if I have grown horns. They've been trying out hairstyles for their upcoming wedding—a double wedding that's only two weeks away—and I'm trying to figure out my life. It seems to have blown up into a raging catastrophe, all thanks to Gracie and that parking lot kiss. Which I didn't hate. I definitely *did not* hate it. But I hate that I don't hate it. I hate more that I think I might want to do it again, which freaks me out even more than the original kiss.

"Why can't you talk to your sister about this again?" May asks. "If they are best friends, maybe she can help you."

"You want me to tell my sister that I kissed her lifelong best friend? She will kill me." I run my hands over my face. "You two are all I've got. You have to help me."

May chuckles. "If she sends any more animals here, John will kill you, and all of your problems will be solved."

"She sent more?" Calliope asks, glancing into the mirror to see what May has done.

"Sheep and a pig. It's insane, but I'd be lying if I said I hate it. John does, but it's kind of fun for me. Still, no more," she says, waving shears at me.

I sigh and stand.

Calliope grasps my hand. "Wait, sit down. We'll try to help. Tell us again how this feud began."

She's sweet, and I'm a lucky guy to have them both as future sisters-in-law, but no one on the planet will be able to figure this out. This thing between Gracie and me has gone on for so long that I can't even remember what started it. Still, I sit and try to focus.

"Gracie has been friends with Nina forever, but sometime in middle school, she decided she hated me."

"I thought you said it started in high school when your snake ate her hamster," May says.

"Well, that didn't help, but the more I think about it, the more I realize we had issues in middle school, too, like around sixth grade or so. Anyway, I always tried to be nice to her, but I wasn't a smart guy. I did stupid things, but whenever I tried to apologize to her, she always..." I motion my hands around because I don't know how to describe Gracie Gallagher. "I don't know, like she was daydreaming or something. It was always so awkward."

May sits in the chair beside Calliope and bites her lip. "Paul, I hate to tell you, but there is clearly a lot you are missing here. I seriously doubt middle and high school miscommunications and pranks are enough for her to despise you enough to fill my home with livestock."

"Once, she paid someone to put laxatives in my sports drink," I say, glaring at her.

Calliope snorts and spews her drink all over herself. "Okay, that stings."

May chuckles and hands her a tissue before giving her attention back to me. "Listen, I think the best thing for you to do is come right out and ask her what the problem is. Talk it out with her, bite your tongue when you want to resort to insults, and if she's still angry, you'll probably have to let it go and move on. I don't know her, so I can't give you anything better than that."

I know she's trying, but she's right. They don't know Gracie like I do. Asking her why she kissed me and why we are fighting will be as successful as adding bleach to my laundry and hoping I don't get spots. I tug my hat over my head and sigh yet again.

"I'll try. I've gotta get home and grade some papers, then catch up on a few documentaries I want to show in class. I appreciate the help, ladies." I stand and stretch, then turn to find John headed to May's little salon in the making. I have no desire to get the third degree again, so I glance at May.

She nods toward the back. "Go on. I'll keep him busy while you scram."

I kiss her cheek, ruffle Calliope's hair, then bolt. I manage to make it out the back just as John enters, dart to my Jeep, and disappear down the drive before he can run me down. The whole way home, I think about my visit to the library. Why on earth was the library torn apart? It looked like a hurricane went through it, but there was no way I'd offer to help clean it up. Edwin would scowl and tell me I should have, but offering such a thing to Gracie would just be more of the same—bleach in the laundry.

Miles down the road, I pass the house Edwin and Calliope just bought and try not to be jealous. Love just fell into my brothers' laps. The perfect woman for them appeared out of thin air, stole their hearts, and their fairy tale weddings were just around the corner. But me? Not a prayer. Not even a single girlfriend in my past came close to the kind of love I see between my brothers and the women they fell for.

Nina swears being single is not a curse. My time will come... but will it? She and I are barely ten months apart, so we've shared a lot, including the same classes for most of our school lives. It wasn't until middle school that we had some time apart, then high school, but our friend circle always ended up being the same group... including Gracie. But the one thing we don't have in common is our marital status. Nina was the first of us to marry, but she and Rhodes knew in fifth grade they would get married. It was only a matter of time.

When I reach my house—a two-bedroom townhouse just outside of the city—it's already dark. I spent more time bugging May and Calliope about Gracie than I care to admit, but it's really bothering me. She called me a whole load of names, and then... she *kissed* me. For a second, I forgot we were arguing. Heck, I forgot my *name*, but when she pulled away and opened her eyes, I saw the clouds roll in. It was like, for a moment, she'd forgotten about the feud, and things were perfect between us. Then she blinked, and a rage monster took over. She smacked me and left me standing in the parking lot dumbfounded, intrigued, and at a total loss for words.

I stare out my windshield. My insides are twisted, and I know it'll be another night of sleeplessness, which isn't entirely fair when none of this is my fault. I check my watch and, like an idiot, decide I have plenty of time to drive to her house, settle this, and get back home to grade those papers. The whole way, I think about what to say. Things like *it was a great kiss, but we shouldn't let it fuel the fight*, less responsible things like *you're a terrible person who is mean to everyone*, and even something worse like *kiss me again.*

Shaking my head clear, I find myself in her driveway. The house is a lot more rundown than I remember. The front porch sags, and it looks like the roof is missing a lot of shingles, but it's hard to tell in the dark. This is probably a bad idea. Scratch that. I know it's a bad idea, but before I put my Jeep in reverse, an angry woman bangs on the driver's side window and scares the snot out of me.

"What are you doing here?" Gracie screams.

I roll down my window and prepare my ears for her tantrum.

"I came to talk to you, but if it's a bad time—"

"Of course, it's a bad time. Did it ever occur to you to call me first? I have mares to feed and settle before I can even think about going to sleep. I'm busy, Paul, and on my list of priorities, you are nowhere near the top."

Well, that stings. I was never under any impression that I was on her priority list at all, but to hear her say aloud that I'm essentially useless to her kind of hurts.

For some reason—because I'm stupid—I salute and put my Jeep in reverse.

"Seriously?" she snaps.

I blink and put my vehicle back in park. "What? I'm confused. You said it was a bad time."

"Yeah, well, you're here now. You might as well help me." She rolls her eyes and walks away, headed back toward the stable. The woman has reached a new level of frustrating, and I can't decide if I should follow her or get out while the getting is good. Naturally, I slam the door behind me and follow her.

It's almost too dark to see anything, but when she steps in front of the barn, a floodlight turns on and illuminates most of the side pasture. It's early spring, but the grass is already high enough to need mowing. I glance toward the barn and notice one door is off the hinges, leaning up against the wall. Gracie was never this messy or disorganized, and I wonder what has happened. Do I ask? Absolutely not.

She's brushing down one of the mares, whose belly is so big there's no denying she's pregnant, and the rhythm seems to calm her. I decide it's probably my turn to talk, and I clear my throat. Gracie pauses, and I hear her soft sigh before she resumes brushing.

"Uh, so I'm sorry about yelling at you earlier. John had chewed me out, and I was angry. I should have stuck around and helped you clean up the library and been more polite in how I spoke to you."

"It's my job. It's fine." She drops the brush and grabs a bucket, then leads the mare into the barn. I have no idea if I'm supposed to follow her, so I wait outside in the dark. It's creepy, and a chill courses down my spine, but there is zero chance I'll admit I'm afraid of the dark and go into the stable. She's liable to decapitate me with a sickle or something if I'm not meant to be in there.

There's clanging and neighing, and then she exits and whistles. Another mare saunters toward her and stands while Gracie gets to work brushing her. There are five more horses in the pasture, and I'm pretty sure she's going to repeat this task until they are all cleaned and fed, so I can either say what I came to say—not that I know what that is—or excuse myself and let her work because whatever I attempt to do to help her, will undoubtedly blow up and go wrong.

I lick my lips and fidget with my keys.

Gracie slows her brushing again and stands straight. She picks at the bristles of the brush, her gaze glued to the ground. All I can really see is her silhouette, but even so, her shoulders are slumped, and she's closed off.

"Listen, I'm sorry about all of the animals. I'll call John myself tomorrow, and if he doesn't want them, I can arrange for new homes."

"Oh, if you think you can get those animals away from May, you're crazy, but it would be great if you could not send more. Their wedding is in two weeks, and she's got enough to do."

"I said I was sorry," she snaps.

I bite back the urge to return the favor and tighten my grip on my keys. "I know you did. I was only clarifying my request." She finally looks at me, but in the dark, I can't make out her expression. I want to, though, because I can't figure her out. Seeing her face won't necessarily help, but at least I'll know if I'm about to lose my head. I step forward until the floodlight turns on again, but she turns away before I can catch a glimpse.

Back to brushing, ignoring me.

"Gracie, can we please talk like adults?"

"About what? I apologized about the animals. I won't send any more, and you apologized for getting so angry. It's all good. Nothing else to talk about."

Her voice wavers. Is she crying?

"Gracie, I think—"

"I'm really busy, Paul."

"So let me help you." I reach for a brush, pretty sure it's not too difficult to groom a horse, but she swats my hand.

"I've got it."

I can't control my annoyance any longer. "Look, I'm trying here, okay? I don't know what I did that got us into this position, but it's getting stupid. Nina is my sister, and I don't want to fight with her best friend. What can I do?"

She turns around and stares at me much the same way that May and Calliope did. Either I am oblivious, or she is confusing. I can't decide which, but what I think doesn't matter. Clearly, she's put way more thought into this feud between us than I have because, in a breath, she's standing in front of me, poking my chest.

"As if you don't know! Are you *kidding* me? You fed my hamster to your snake!"

"It was an accident!" I shout as she backs me across the small dirt road between the grooming area and the stable.

"Sure, fine, but what about my birthday party? You never would have apologized for shoving me into the pool if your mother hadn't made you. I was teased *relentlessly* over flashing half the kids from school!"

"It was like ten kids, Gracie, not the whole school," I say. Big mistake.

"Well, the whole school found out about it and teased me for months!" she screeches. "And your mom had to force you to apologize. That's the worst part, Paul. You didn't even care."

My eyes went wide. "I lied about my mom, okay? I wanted to apologize, but when I saw you face to face, I didn't know what to say!"

Her eyes narrow, but she doesn't back down. I have about two feet of space before I'm up against a stable, and there's a good chance I'll get skewered by a pitchfork.

She practically growls. It's not believable, I know, but I really wanted to apologize.

"My diary!" She screeches so loudly that her horse whinnies and steps aside.

"What are you even talking about?" I ask, my hands up in defense as she continues to poke my sternum.

"Don't you dare act like you don't remember. You read it and told Stephen Andrews that I had a crush on him! *Everyone* teased me. He was the most popular guy in the whole school, and I had no chance with him. But no, you didn't even consider how it would hurt me, and you told him!"

"First of all, it was Austin who found your diary, not me. I don't even know why you left it in Nina's room, but he was the one who found it. I actually tried to—"

"I don't believe you. Why would your best friend be in Nina's room looking under her bed?"

I smirk. "I think it's obvious. He had a thing for her."

She nearly gags. I get it. Austin did that to people. He had a sick sense of humor, which is partially why we are no longer friends. That, and we went to different states for college and drifted apart. I chuckle, and this reminds her that she's scolding me.

Gracie steps forward again. "Fine, but what was with the thing under the bleachers?"

The bleachers? The bleachers... What happened under the bleachers? I swallow and think back like my life depends on it.

She sighs. "You found me crying under the bleachers and told me Stephen didn't deserve me."

Oh yeah...

"Well, he didn't. I only told him you liked him because I thought he would be smart enough to do something about it. I didn't know he was really as stupid as he seemed."

"You said Stephen read my diary, not you." Her eyes flame... oops.

"Well, he might have shared some things with me, but that's beside the point. I felt bad because I really did think he'd ask you out."

This seems to ease her poking, but I'm still back against a wall here. I'm scared to death that I might say the wrong thing and incur her full wrath. Out here, she could bury my body, and the authorities would never find me. Still, it feels like we might be on the verge of some kind of truce, so I wait patiently while she ponders these things.

Only every single time I blink, she gets more beautiful. She's got hay in her hair, and it's a hot mess. There are strands of it falling out of her bun all over, and she's got dirt smudged on her cheeks. The floodlight isn't flattering, but that's a good thing. If she got any prettier, I'd be in a lot of trouble. More than I already am.

Gracie steps back and gives me some breathing room.

"What about SAT day?"

Oh, that was bad.

"Would you believe me if I said it was an accident, and I definitely did not mean to screw that up for you?"

She narrows her eyes, but rather than respond, she asks, "The purple hair?"

Okay, that was on purpose. I grin even though I know it's going to get me into trouble. "It was a dare, but I am sorry. I was not the smartest kid back then."

She's going to go through every single thing that ever went wrong. I know it, but I'm not expecting what she says next.

"What happened at prom?"

Huh?

My confusion must be evident on my face because she rolls her eyes and sighs. "Never mind. I forgive you for all of those things, but I have to get things done here."

She steps away, but I know I won't sleep if I don't know what she's talking about. I grab her hand and tug her back, forcing her to stumble over her own feet. She recovers fast and grumbles. "What about prom? What do you mean?"

She arches her eyebrows. "The dancing? The niceness? The... The almost... dancing."

"You said dancing twice. And what about it? You were sad, and I wanted to be nice. Is that a crime?"

"Oh," she whispers and lowers her gaze to the ground. "I guess... I misunderstood what... I mean, thank you. I didn't know that. Anyway, I really should finish up."

She lifts her gaze to meet mine, and I realize I haven't released her hand yet. She also doesn't make a move to pull away. Is this a truce? Are we officially ending our years-long argument and moving on? I let go and push off the stable wall, but the boards give out behind me. I fall backward and grab for anything I can get my hands on to keep from smashing onto the ground. Unfortunately, Gracie is the closest thing, and I pull her down with me *through* the barn wall.

Chapter Three
Gracie

GOING THROUGH A BARN wall feels a lot like getting hit by a truck, only I land on Paul, so at least my landing isn't as hard as his. All the breath leaves his body in a whoosh beneath me, and then he wheezes in a sad attempt to reinflate his lungs. I roll off of him as quickly as possible and make sure he hasn't been impaled. He stares at the ceiling of the barn, his eyes darting like he might be a little confused after cracking his skull on the concrete foundation.

"Are you okay?" I ask, scared to move him.

He inhales and rolls on his side, and I just now notice his arm is wrapped around my waist. He protected me, and I don't know how to feel about it.

"Been better. Sorry about the wall." He pushes into a seated position and shifts onto his knees but wobbles and sits back down.

"Are you dizzy?"

"I'll be alright. Are you okay? Did you hit your head or anything?"

"A little, but not too hard," I admit, rubbing the sore spot on my forehead. "I'll survive, but we better get you to a hospital if you can't stand up."

"No, thank you. I've had concussions before. I'll be fine." He lets the words slip out like a brain injury is nothing more than a slight inconvenience and tries to stand again. This time, he makes it to his feet without a problem. "I think I was just disoriented a minute ago. I feel fine."

Famous last words, but I'm not going to argue with him. He's going to do what he wants regardless of my opinion on the matter. Paul offers his hand to help me stand, but I'm already halfway there on my own, so I pretend I don't notice and brush the dirt from my pants. A quick glance, and I know I'm in trouble. It's warming up, but it's still a bit chilly for the mares to be without shelter, and I don't trust the stable now that half of a wall has fallen in.

My eyes burn with the sting of tears because I truly have no idea what I'm going to do. I can't afford to repair the structure, let alone build a new one. Besides that, what in the world will I do with seven mares, one of which is pregnant?

Paul says nothing while I scan the area, my brain in overdrive as I try to work out the logistics of moving seven horses somewhere safe and warm. I sigh and run my hands over my face.

"I don't know what to do," I admit, letting my arms fall back to my sides. "I don't know what to do anymore."

Paul takes a step forward to stand beside me and takes in the full devastation. Even in the dark, it's a horrible mess. He tugs on my sleeve.

"We should get your horse and get out of here before the whole thing collapses. That roof does not look sturdy." His eyes are glued to the ceiling, and he's not wrong. It's been in need of repair for some time, but without the full support of all four walls, it sags even more.

I grab a lead and clip it to Anastasia, my oldest mare, and lead her out of the building. I despise the thought of Paul seeing me here at my worst, but it isn't as if he hasn't seen me in the dumps before. Even so, my home and property have gotten much worse since he last saw it at least three years ago. Its state is embarrassing, but without money, there's not much I can do. I've tried to fix what I can a little at a time, but it's falling apart faster than I can fix it.

"Uh, do you have another stable or something?" he asks, trying to see out over my property for a hidden building somewhere.

"No. I guess I'll have to trailer them one at a time, drive across town to my vet, and hope she has enough room for them until I can figure something out."

Paul checks his watch. "It's late. It'll take you all night to do that. Why don't I call John and see if he can help us? His stable is huge."

"No, but thanks," I snap. The last thing I need is to impose on John and his fiancé any more than I already have. What was I thinking? Messing with John to get back at Paul was unwise, but realizing that now does not solve my current problem. In fact, it probably makes it worse.

"Too late," he says and crams his phone in his pocket. "I already asked. He's gonna let me borrow his trailer. I'll go pick it up and help you move them to their property for now. There's room."

"For seven horses? Even with all of the animals I sent over there?" I do not remember how big John's property is, but I have a feeling I'm about to bump it up to maximum capacity.

"Yep. May has big plans, and if May wants it, she gets it. John is like a little puppy these days."

I look at Anastasia, my poor, tired girl, and give in. Transporting the horses to John's place will take less time and cause less trauma than a long trip across town. It's still going to take forever, but at least my babies won't be as stressed.

Still, it's an imposition of epic proportions, and I haven't even met May. She probably hates me after everything I've done, which will make this a lot of trouble. I'm so embarrassed, I'm blushing. Thank goodness Paul can't see it in the dark, even with the floodlight.

"It's a huge imposition, and I'm sure—"

"Gracie, you're family. You have been since we were kids. Sure, we get into squabbles, but at the end of the day, you are Nina's best friend. I'm sure May will be excited her ponies will have a few friends."

I swallow the lump in my throat. *Family.* Yeah, if Nina ever forgives me. It's been a few weeks since we've spent time together, which isn't completely unusual since we are both busy, but usually, there are some texting or voice messages between us until we can talk again. But now... nothing. She's still furious about the kiss, and I don't blame her. It was a stupid thing to do.

"I'll be back in a few," Paul says.

"Wait, there's no sense in not taking one of them along. I'll get Anastasia loaded and follow you. I should apologize to John before loading him up with more animals."

Paul nods and waits for me to gather what I need. Most of the gals haven't eaten yet, so I pray they have hay and load a few bags of grain in my truck along with the necessary supplies to hold us over until tomorrow. When I start to load Anastasia, Paul steps forward. I raise my hand to hold him off.

"It's fine. I've got it. She's a good loader, but you might scare her." True to my word, Anastasia loads like a charm.

Paul runs a hand through his hair before stuffing it in his pocket. I hate how adorable he is, just like he was when we were in high school. Not much has changed about him except those muscles, of course, but otherwise, he's still the same guy. I can tell myself all day long that I hate him and stay mad about all of the stupid things that happened between us, but at the end of the day, the truth is the truth. I've been crazy about Paul for a long, long time.

I brush the hair from my face and dig my keys from my pocket. "I guess I'm ready. Thank you for helping me with this. It'll take half as long."

"Thank goodness tomorrow is Saturday, right?" he asks and flashes me that stinking grin of his.

"You say that like the library is closed on Saturday. I still have to work," I say and open my truck door. He hasn't made a single motion to get into his Jeep. He's walking closer to me in the opposite direction of his vehicle.

"Maybe I can help? Did that whole mess already get cleaned up, or do you need a hand?"

I arch my eyebrow and tilt my head. "It's clean. I mean, we have someone coming to clean the carpet in the morning, but otherwise, it's ready for people again."

Paul leans on my truck, cornering me between his body and the door. I can easily get *into* the vehicle, but... I don't want to. This is different. There's less tension between us at the moment. We've managed to say more than three sentences to one another without screaming or fussing, so we're already onto a record. It would be a shame to interfere with such things, so I lean against my door and cross my arms.

"Did you get the World War II exhibit fixed?"

"It is in chronological order, yes. What does that have to do with anything we need to do right now?" I ask, tilting my head back to look up at him. He steps forward and grins again. Heaven help me, that Loughton grin. No one can ever say the brothers can't reel the girls in with a well-placed smirk or grin. In fact, Paul's ability to flash that smile and have a flock of girls trailing after him was unparalleled in high school—another thing that made me angry almost all the time.

"Nothing. I was just asking." He takes a deep breath. "Since I kind of have you at my mercy right now, I'm going to take a chance and ask you something that you're not going to want to answer."

Oh, no. He's not wrong. I'm cornered, and I need his brother's stable. I'm in no position to sass my way out of what he's about to ask me, and I know exactly what it is. I swallow, and Paul inches closer still. There's so little space between us now I'm pretty sure we'd break the personal space rule from high school ten times over. An inch or so is all that separates me from complete humiliation at his hands.

He takes another breath. "Gracie, please tell me the truth. Why did you kiss me in the parking lot?"

My throat seizes, and all I want is for lightning to strike me where I stand. I can't tell him the truth. How can I say that the kiss was everything I had ever wanted but that it was so impulsive I didn't even realize I had done it until it was happening? How can I tell him that, despite everything that has happened between us, I still want more than anything for him to look at me like he sees me, really *sees* me as a woman he could love and not just his sister's best friend?

I lick my lips, a lie formulating as high beams flash into my driveway. Paul leaps back from me, and I breathe a sigh of relief. Evidently, John decided to take matters into his own hands. He's brought a trailer, and now we can get this show on the road—the horse relocation show, not the one where I admit that Paul's very presence makes me giddy like a schoolgirl all over again. Bleh. That will never happen. There is no chance I'm ever admitting that, not when I am the least desirable person in the world to him.

"He's so impatient," Paul says and sighs. He glances at me and reaches for my chin. He grasps it and tilts my head back, sending a jolt of anxiety through me. The good kind. The kind that makes a person woozy with excitement. "Don't think for one second that I'm going to forget about that conversation we need to have. I want to know why you kissed me. The truth, Gracie, and I'm not going to stop bugging you until you tell me."

She inhales as if to speak, then high-tails it out of my reach.

Chapter Four

Paul

I'VE MADE A THREAT I cannot back up, and Gracie knows it. If she decides to keep her secret to the grave, there will be no getting it out of her. Still, I kind of hope she'll tell me the truth so we can move on with our truce on less shaky ground.

"That's the last of them," Gracie says.

John lets out a long exhale and runs his hands over his face. I'm gonna catch a ton of his frustration over this, but it's not entirely my fault his house is full of farm animals and now all of Gracie's horses. Hopefully, the latter can be rectified soon.

"I'm so sorry to be such an imposition. I can definitely call my vet tomorrow and make better arrangements," Gracie says, her hair sticking out everywhere after several hours of work.

"No, it's perfectly fine," May says. "John says you're like family, so it's not a problem for you to keep them here. Just focus on getting your home fixed up, and don't worry about anything here."

Gracie sighs in relief. "Thank you. I really appreciate it so much." She pets her pregnant mare once more then digs her keys from her pocket. "I should head home. I have a shift at the library tomorrow, but it's only half a day. I can come by and take care of the afternoon routine."

May smiles when the horse nuzzles her cheek. "It's fine. I enjoy spending time out here."

"They're all very gentle and shouldn't give you any problems. Spice might be a little naughty, but if you're firm, she'll back down. The pregnant one isn't due for another month." Gracie doesn't want to leave her horses, which is clear in her stature, but she finally drops her hand and jingles her keys. "Give me a call if there are any issues. Thanks again."

John glances at me with an indecipherable expression. Maybe he's sick thinking about how his house has turned into a three-ring circus, but it's probably something more along the lines of wanting me to drop dead so he can feed me to his pig and be done with my drama. I nod and walk alongside Gracie back to our vehicles.

The silence is loud, so I break it by clearing my throat.

The screen door slams and I glance over my shoulder. John and May have disappeared into the house, leaving me in the dark with Gracie. The porch light is faint but enough to illuminate the walkway to her truck.

"Do you need help with anything else before I head home?" I ask, fidgeting with my keys. Literally, any word I say could incite a riot, so I try to choose carefully.

"No, thank you. You've done enough," she says, averting her gaze. "Thank you for arranging this with John. It would have been miserable to take them all across town."

I shrug. "Well, it was sort of my fault your entire wall crashed in. I can pay for—"

"No, no." Gracie's gaze catches mine, and she shakes her head almost violently. "It isn't your fault it fell. It's been on its last legs for a long time. I'm just glad you're not hurt. Are you sure your head is okay?" She reaches for my head, then yanks her hand back, almost as if she remembered she's supposed to hate me. She pulls her lips into a firm line.

"I'm alright. Good thing since I've been driving." I chuckle and twirl my keys. I know I should let her go home to get some sleep, and I definitely should do the same, but I can't stop thinking about the state of her home and what it might mean. She was only nineteen when she bought it, having saved every penny from her part-time job during high school to earn a down payment. She's the hardest worker I know, and she never asks for anything. At least, that's what Nina always says. But there is every chance in the world she is in over her head.

"I should—"

"Gracie, are—"

She huffs a little laugh and says, "Go ahead."

I step forward and find it impossible to stop myself from grasping her elbow. When she stiffens, I let my hand slip down her arm to grasp her hand. "Are you okay? Is there anything I can—"

"I'm fine," she snaps and pulls her hand free. She inhales and turns towards her truck. "Goodnight, Paul." She's inside the safety of her vehicle before I can stop her or formulate any rational argument as to why she *shouldn't* stay and talk to me, so I release a frustrated groan and head home.

After a less-than-restful night, I stare at my ceiling, wondering what to do with myself on a Saturday besides grade papers that will all disappoint me. I have exactly one student who pays attention, and it's only so she can try to catch me with incorrect facts. She's failed with every attempt, but it's fun to watch her try to play the gotcha game with a lifelong history buff.

I check my phone and roll out of bed. John has already threatened my life in three separate messages, but I'm certain his worry that he just acquired seven new horses is unfounded. Gracie loves those beasts, and there is no way they will be at John's house permanently. How long, though, remains a question. The barn is demolished, and if the state of disrepair of the exterior of her home is any indication, she either can't afford to fix anything or doesn't have time.

I have to fix it.

It's kind of my fault anyway, no matter what she claims, so I decide that's what I will do with my day. After a quick shower and breakfast, I head over to the hardware store and the lumber yard. It's an obscene amount of money because, I was informed, lumber costs had gone up considerably. I have no idea what they were before, but that doesn't help me much now.

With a truck full of boards and supplies, I head back to Gracie's house. I know she's at the library, so I can at least get some of the work out of the way in peace and quiet, free from trying to figure out the woman.

In the light of day, it's obvious it's more than a wall that will need to be replaced. The whole thing is a pile of junk just waiting to collapse, which is well beyond my purview. I'm handy with a hammer, but not *that* handy. Instead of spending my time on that project, I turn to the front porch. There is no sense in wasting the lumber, so I begin pulling cracked and broken boards from the porch and replacing them with bright, shiny new ones. After the porch repairs, I walk around the property to see what else needs to be done. Mowing... I hop on the tractor and get started, only once pausing to consider that she might kill me for being on her property without her permission.

This task takes a while, but it's pleasant, and I don't notice how much time passes until Gracie pulls into her driveway and parks beside my truck. I guide the tractor down the hill and park it, cut the engine, and pray she doesn't lose her ever-loving mind that I decided to spend my day doing random chores at her house.

I should have asked first.

That thought tumbles around in my mind while I watch her slam her car door closed, stomp up to me, and put her hands on her hips.

"What are you doing?"

I run my hand through a sweaty mop of hair and try to grin my way out of this. "Mowing," I say. "I was just about to gather it all up for the horses unless you usually leave it."

"Uh... I gather it, but... why are you mowing, exactly?"

I shrug. "Doesn't look like you've had time. You're busy, and I had free time, so I thought I'd help."

"But... why?" She tilts her head the same way May's dog, Frisco, does, and I worry she might bite just as hard.

I'm about to say I felt like I should after destroying her barn when she catches a glimpse of her porch.

"You fixed the porch?" she whines. "Paul, I was saving up to do that. I don't have the money to pay for—"

"Wait," I say, slipping from the tractor. "I wanted to repair the mess I made of the barn, but when I saw it, I realized I couldn't fix that. I fixed the porch instead. Gracie, you don't owe me anything."

She eyes me up and down, and I don't miss how her gaze lingers on my lips a blink longer than it should. She clears her throat and sighs. "Well... thank you. I don't know what I'll do about the barn. I probably need to tear it down and build another one, but that will cost a ton of money I just don't have on a librarian's salary."

"I'm sure May and John won't mind keeping the horses for a while. Do you have any idea what it will cost?" I wince because, judging by how much I spent on what little I bought today, I'm sure it's not a pleasing number.

She scoffs and says, "The estimate for one just barely large enough was over forty thousand."

I choke on my own spit, which brings a chuckle to her lips. It only lasts for a second, and she walks away towards the barn.

"I wonder if I can salvage anything, and it might cost less?" She walks around it, taking stock of her own hot mess for a minute before glancing at me like I might know. There's so much hope in her gaze that I can't think of anything realistic to say.

Instead, I say, "Maybe. I can help you try if you want."

She narrows those pretty blue eyes of hers, and I catch the smattering of freckles over the bridge of her nose. I used to tease her about those, but now I kind of like them. I don't know why I like the freckles on my mortal enemy's nose, but I do, and it's all I can look at while she stares back at me, expecting something more... like a punchline. I think I might like to kiss those freckles, but since that thought makes me panic, I shut it down and refocus.

"The doors look good, and the window moldings. I see a lot of boards that look solid. I actually think there's more salvageable than I did when I first looked at it. Do you know anyone who can pull it apart?"

She finally pulls her gaze away from me and scans the barn. "Actually, I do. I think my neighbor might be willing to do a trade for the baby."

"Uh... what?"

She laughs again. "The mare that's pregnant is his favorite. If I give the foal to him, he would probably demo this for me for free. Let me text him and see if he can come by." She pulls out her phone and sends a message, then gives her attention back to me. "Thank you for this. I, um... I guess I should apologize again for everything."

Her shoulders sag, and I wonder if this is finally it. Is this the moment when we start acting like adults and stop torturing each other for no reason at all? Well, she has reasons, but I kind of think they are all ridiculous. We were kids, and while that is no excuse for some of my behavior, I'm not the only one to blame. She pulled her fair share of stunts that made me furious.

I cram my hands in my pockets. "I mean, I'm sorry, too. We've both been kind of ridiculous. Friends?"

She gives me some serious side-eye and purses her lips. "I wouldn't go that far, but at least not enemies. I'll stop rolling my eyes when I hear your name and play nice in front of other people."

She rolls her sleeves up and shields her eyes from the intense sunlight beating down on us. I'm just about to suggest we chat on the porch rather than in the field when another car pulls into the drive.

"Oh, there's Christian, my neighbor." She makes a beeline toward his car, leaving me behind.

Christian steps out of his car, and some sort of pre-historic, ape-man, green-eyed monster crawls up from the depths of my gut, and the primal urge to claim Gracie as *mine* eats me up. This so-called neighbor of hers has clearly been ripped from the pages of an athletic gear catalog. He's wearing a rugby uniform, and even though the shorts are way too short for any man to wear, I have to admit those muscles are as thick as stupid trees—stupid, beetle-ridden, I hope they rot and die trees. He's a beast as it is. Then he opens his mouth, and that Irish accent hits my ears.

I throw my hands in the air and get back on the tractor. Why do I even care? I'll tell you why... I don't know. All I know is her Irish rugby-playing, tree trunks-for-legs neighbor is not my competition. Or I should say, there is no chance I am any competition for him. Gracie giggles and smacks his arm, and I almost lean over the side of the tractor to hurl. Instead, I start it up to interrupt their conversation like the fully grown adult man that I am.

Gracie throws a glare over her shoulder, and the two head to her porch—the one I just repaired for her. By the time I'm across the field to put the tractor back into the shed, the two of them are wandering around the barn, pointing and laughing. Stupid neighbor.

I'm acting like a jealous boar, as Edwin would call it, but I can't help it. I also can't figure it out. Pre-kiss, I would never have given Gracie a second thought, not in the ways I'm thinking about her now. But since I can't decipher how I feel, this behavior makes no sense.

I swallow the lump in my throat and turn off the tractor, then head towards my truck. I know ignoring her, and Mr. Supermodel is rude. I'm acting like a jerk, but I can't figure out why I feel this way, and it's kind of freaking me out. I unlock my truck, and Gracie calls for me.

"Paul! Are you leaving?"

"Uh... I didn't want to interfere," I say. Lies. I'm a jealous idiot, and I don't want to admit it.

"Come here," she calls and waves me over.

I heave a sigh and head over toward the barn while swallowing my pride. It's not doing me a bit of good anyway, and there is every chance that this guy is perfectly nice. It's not his fault I've been in a lifelong feud with his neighbor, who probably thinks he's hot... or something.

She smiles when I stop a few feet away from them and says, "Christian says he can break it down and salvage a lot."

"Yeah, it should be no problem, but I could use a hand. Do you mind?" Christian asks. He doesn't give me a chance to answer before he adds, "My wife just had a baby, so I have to check in on her from time to time. Having an extra hand here would make the work go faster."

Oh, thank you, Lord. He's married, and a father, and his smile hit his eyes when he spoke about them. The weight of an elephant—the one in the room that only I saw—lifted from my chest.

"You don't have to," Gracie says. "I know you're busy, and we're... you know. So, if you can't, then I can try to ask my cousins or someone."

For reasons only the primal beast inside of me knows, I reach up and brush my thumb over her cheek, caressing those freckles I want to kiss. "Of course, I'll help. I don't mind."

Christian doesn't miss a beat. He smacks me on the shoulder and says, "Great. We can start in an hour. Will that be alright?"

I nod but can't peel my eyes away from Gracie. Her lips part and she stares back at me, and I just keep rubbing that spot under her eye because I'm not sure what else to do now. Christian disappears back into his car and down the lane, and still, we're staring at each other.

She finally blinks and breaks the trance, but the tension is too thick to ignore. I seize the opportunity, because I don't know when I will catch her this cheerful again. "Gracie—"

"No." She shakes her head and pulls away. "No, just... not now, Paul. I can't right now."

Without another word, she hurries into her house and closes the door behind her.

Chapter Five

Gracie

CHRISTIAN AND HIS WIFE are the best neighbors a girl can ask for, but when Christian goes back home for the night, I'm left in awkward silence with Paul, sorting boards that we will keep versus get rid of. It's dusk now, and soon Paul will head home, which gives me both comfort and indigestion. I want him to be near me, but I'm also sure that I'm going to have to explain that kiss sooner or later.

An hour into the demolition, Christian asked me if Paul and I were dating. When I said we weren't, he chuckled but did not elaborate. I wanted to ask what made him ask such a crazy question, but I was too embarrassed that even my neighbor had picked up on the tension between Paul and me.

Paul runs his hands through his hair for the tenth time in an attempt to keep it out of his face.

"You should ask May to give you a haircut. She seems really sweet," I say, trying to initiate a meaningless conversation to fill the void before he dives into interrogation mode again.

"She is sweet. She's supposed to cut it for me later this week. She's just been busy with her sister planning." He tosses a few rotted boards into the ever-growing pile and maneuvers around to the next stack. His flipping muscles are making me a little weak in the knees, I admit. He was never gangly or scrawny, not that any of the Loughton boys ever were, but Paul was built more like an athlete than his brothers. Edwin has always been slender, while John was more like a bulldozer. Paul is that sweet spot in between.

He glances at me and catches me staring. That stupid grin pops, and he says, "Why don't you take a picture? It'll last you longer."

"Oh, my gosh, are we in school again?" I ask with my cheeks on fire.

He tosses another board and smiles wider. "Nope. We're all grown up now."

"Mmm, I'm not so sure about you being a grown-up." I run my hands over my face to hide the fact that they are on fire. The good thing is it helps. The bad thing is, when I drop my hands, Paul is standing right in front of me. He's sweaty, and his hair sticks up all over, but it's hard to notice those things because he's grinning and staring down at me with an *I'm up to something* expression. I back up a step and trip over the small pile of boards behind me.

"Where do you think you're going?" Paul catches me around the waist and keeps me from falling, but I think

I would have rather suffered the splinters and cuts from landing in a pile of boards over being in his arms like this. It isn't that I don't *want* to be. Heaven knows it's getting harder and harder for me to deny my attraction to my nemesis... former nemesis, maybe... but there's nothing between us. I remind myself of that and wiggle free.

"Uh, I should probably clean up and figure out what I'm going to do for dinner."

Paul releases me and steps over the boards beside me, wiping his hands on his pants. "What are you going to make us?"

I freeze so fast I almost trip again, this time over my own feet. "Us?"

He shrugs. "Sure. I mean, I did stick around and help demolish a giant barn today. I'm a growing boy who worked up an appetite, Gracie. Feed me, or I might die." He dramatically throws himself at me, but I sidestep, and he trips over the same boards I almost fell into. He contorts himself so he lands on his rear end and scowls up at me, but it doesn't last. He spackles on that stupid, *flirty* grin again. "Let me take you to dinner. May is taking care of the horses. You worked hard today, and you should have a break."

I can't help but wonder what his sudden kindness means. One, the obvious—why is Paul Loughton asking me to dinner? And two, what do I do? I want to say yes, please take me to dinner and fall wildly in love with me just as I have always dreamed, but the scared part of me withdraws and hides back in her huddle hole.

Unfortunately, the scared part of me wins, and I put on an aloof, cold face.

"No, thank you. No dining with Paul Loughton," I say with a scowl.

"Are you saying no because you don't want to talk about the thing I want to talk about or because the thought of dining with me gives you stomach cramps?" he teases.

"I'm saying no because I'm tired," I whisper, trying to control my emotions. Scowling at him doesn't seem to do the trick anymore, so perhaps partial honesty will.

His grin falters, and he nods. "Okay, well, I guess I'll see you around. Christian said he could finish up on his own." He stands and brushes his pants off again, but it's different now. He's closed off and in a rush. Somehow, I've hurt him, but I don't think it's because I turned down dinner with him. It's something else. It's that silly kiss, and it really is eating him up as much as it is me.

"Paul?" I barely hear my own voice, but he pauses, checking his pockets for his keys to give me his attention. "I... I'm not..." I bite my lip and finally blurt it all out. "I'm not trying to be difficult about the kiss. I just don't *know* why I did it. Can you give me some time to sort out my feelings? I promise, I'll tell you when I know."

His throat bobs, and his eyes roam my face as if he's never seen me before, but he nods. "Yes. I can wait. And I'm not trying to be a jerk about it, but I'm not sure why I kissed you back, either. I'm confused and... yeah, confused."

"I know. I promise I'm trying," I admit.

He lowers his gaze to his shoes and finally finds his keys. "I know, Gracie. This is just the beast we made, and now we have to reckon with it, I guess. Let me know if you need more help, okay?" He hardly looks at me when he waves and says goodbye. He's in his truck and backing down the drive before I let myself relax. Even then, my gut is twisted, and I have to fight the urge to run after him.

What am I doing? He's trying to bridge this gap between us, for whatever reason, and all I'm doing is cutting him off at every turn. My throat hurts. Tears well in my eyes. I inhale and watch his truck disappear over the hill and out of view. I can call him back, send him a message, and tell him I changed my mind, but it will only lead to heartache and abandonment. Love always does, and I don't think my heart can handle being broken that way, not by him.

Instead, I head inside and shower, grab a quick bite—spaghetti again—and sit on my sofa to call Nina. She's given me the silent treatment for long enough, but I know why. I know she's worried about me and her brother, and she's only trying to protect us both. I swallow the lump in my throat and send her a message asking her to please call me, that I miss her desperately and need to talk to her. My whole life is on the verge of spiral. I feel it, sense it coming from miles away because I've been here before.

When my biological parents left me, it destroyed me. Sure, I have amazing adoptive parents, but when my birth parents left me at five years old... I clamp my eyes shut and try not to think about how two people can claim to love someone, a small child for five years, then walk away and never look back. There was no addiction, no desperation, no poverty that should have brought them to that. They should have tried everything to keep me, but they didn't. Their habits were more important than me, and that was the cold, hard truth of it.

My phone rings, startling me back to the present. I take a deep breath and answer.

"Hey. Thanks for calling."

Nina sighs. "I missed you too. I'm on my way, and I'll be there in a few minutes, okay?"

"Yeah, okay," I say and hang up. I have a few minutes to pick up and straighten my living room and kitchen before she arrives. I know she won't abandon me the way my parents did, but the fear still consumes me. Nina was the only reason I survived when I was old enough to know why my parents really left me, not the sugar-coated story my adoptive parents wanted me to know. They meant well. They truly did, but grappling with abandonment issues while also going through high school drama was not a good time.

She knocks then opens the door, hands full of junk food neither of us should eat if we intend to stay healthy. I smile, and tears slip free. Nina drops everything onto the sofa and engulfs me in a hug so tight I can't breathe.

"Hey, I'm sorry, okay? I'm not mad at you anymore. I'm never going anywhere, and you know it." She smooths my hair and pulls back to look at me. "But we seriously need to talk about you and my brother."

I try to laugh through the tears, but it's not working. "Your friendship means more to me than anything. I would never intentionally do something to anger you, and I honestly cannot say why I kissed him. I just—"

"Please, I know why. Gracie, I've known why for years, but for some reason, you keep pretending your feelings for him don't exist, even when I call you on it." She gives me her signature *I know you better than you know yourself* stare down. My bestie is the most gorgeous woman in the whole world, and even that look doesn't diminish her beauty, though it does twist my stomach. "Just tell him how you feel."

"I can't do that," I say and head back into the kitchen to make us a pot of coffee.

"Yes, you can. You kissed him, so I would think a conversation about said kiss would be less awkward than the actual kiss." She pushes her long dark hair over her shoulder and leans against my counter.

"You're funny, you know that? He's such a flirt, and there is no way to know how he feels, so I am most definitely *not* going to put myself out there to get humiliated, but thanks."

"He flirts when he's nervous. I don't think he even knows he's doing it, and you know that."

"Right, but he doesn't flirt with *me*," I remind her.

She throws her hands in the air and scowls. "Because he knows you! He's known you for as long as I have, Gracie. There's no reason for him to be nervous around you, but that doesn't mean you shouldn't at least try."

"And when it fails, I lose you both. Perfect example, you got mad and ignored me for weeks after I admitted to kissing him."

Her lips turn down, and she sighs. "Gracie, I was worried about all of this, but I've had a lot of time to think about it. If it's what you want, I won't stand in the way. Just don't lie to Paul or lead him on. He's not the same as Edwin and John. He's... he's... things hit him harder, okay?"

I huff and pull out a chair. "You say that like I don't know him at all."

"Do you?" Nina sits across from me while the pot brews. "He was here today, wasn't he? The front porch is repaired, and I know you don't have time or money for those things."

I roll my eyes and sit back. "You know, it's still creepy how you know everything. Honestly, it's like you have a tap into all of the gossip, and you just *know* before anyone else."

She arches a perfect eyebrow and says, "Look, I understand everything with your birth parents and how much it bothered you when we were younger, but at some point, you have to realize that not everyone leaves, Gracie. Your adoptive parents travel a lot, but they call you all the time and visit often. I haven't left, and I won't, but I am not enough to fill your life. Some day, you'll need to let your guard down and let someone else in."

"Not Paul." I put my foot down now. "There's too much at stake, and I'm not going there." It's all lies because I want him more than anything. There are

exactly zero men in the world who come close to what
Paul means to me, but I can't pinpoint why that is.
Maybe the silly crush I'd had in middle school only
grew stronger and stronger until now all I can feel
was this all-consuming emotion for him. It's not quite
love because how can you love someone you fight with
constantly? But it's something like it, and it's tangled up
in all of those fears that people never stay. That even
Nina will probably leave someday. That I can only trust
myself, and it's better to be alone.

Nina is quiet for a while but eventually relents. "Fine,
but you better make it clear to him, and sooner rather
than later. Discuss the kiss, get it over with, and move
on before someone gets hurt." I don't miss how her tone
comes across as a soft threat. She loves her brothers.
I've been witness to her running off more than one
unworthy woman, and a thought strikes me. She gave
me permission to pursue her brother. Whether I would
or not doesn't matter. Nina thought I was worthy of him,
and that thought warms my heart enough to make me
smile.

She raises an eyebrow again.

"I'll talk to him. Things were really civil last night and
today, and I'd like to be friends with him without all the
drama. I think we're past all of the junk anyway. We're
adults now, right?"

The coffee maker beeps to alert us that the coffee is
ready, so I stand to get us cups.

"Alright, enough of the boy drama. Let's watch some
movies, gossip about celebrities, and pretend we're rich

and famous," Nina says, throwing her hands in the air. The rest of the night will be filled with laughter and bonding, just like it has been for years. We're good, and that's all I could have asked for.

I grab some cookies and chocolate and head into the living room, where she's already getting things set up. While I am glad my best friend and I have mended fences, my mind drifts towards her brother despite trying hard to block him out. I should just tell him kissing him was silly, that it meant nothing, and I'm sorry for everything. If he pushes, I'll tell him I was messing with him, and it backfired. It's all I've got because the truth simply will not cut it, not this time, not if I want to keep Nina in my life.

The reality that Paul will never, ever be mine stings. It isn't as if I ever thought he might be, but this feels a lot more like a period at the end of the dream. It's over. Thousands of diary entries later, hundreds of pranks between us, and this is it. He'll find someone great, get married, and probably have a bunch of kids. I'll breed horses and live with cats, probably, but it's okay. At least I know I can depend on myself. I just have to tell my heart that and hope it listens.

Chapter Six
Paul

NOTHING SAYS LICKING WOUNDS like lurking into church, jealous of your own brothers. My brothers approach with their fiancés, and all I can think about is how badly I want what they have. But I'm heading into church, the last place a guy should behave in such a way. Mom and Dad are already inside, but I'm not ready to sit through the inevitable questions—why haven't you settled down yet? Got your eye on a wife yet? Three down and one to go!

I'm staring at the clouds, wondering if it will rain, when Nina slips her arm in mine and tugs. "I need to talk to you after church." It's all she says, so I'm pretty sure I'm in deep trouble. I don't know what I did, exactly, but she's got that tone that says I've done something atrocious, and I'm gonna pay for it seven different ways. I glance at Rhodes, but he just shrugs, which isn't the best help. We're just on time, so I don't get a chance to drill either of them for information before the service begins.

All through church, my mind wanders. I keep trying to focus on what our pastor says, but I can't help spending the time praying instead. I suppose if a guy is going to tune out the Sunday service, the least he can do is pray. I ask for someone, a woman God chooses for me, and I ask if He could please make it *super* clear when I find her because I'm kind of a dunce when it comes to women. I can't help it that they all make me nervous, and I catch myself saying things I shouldn't.

Mom elbows me a few times, and Edwin catches my eye. He's less grumpy with Calliope, and I can't decipher his expression. I think it's happiness, but it's hard to know since he's usually scowling. Once the last song is sung, I try to escape before Nina can catch me. If I'm nowhere to be found, then maybe I can avoid the lecture until dinner time. That gives me a few hours to come up with a defense, though I'm not sure what I did wrong.

"I've gotta pick up the roast for dinner. Take me by the house?" Nina asks, grasping the back of my suit jacket. Dang it.

"What about Rhodes?" I ask, hoping it will buy me some time if she has to drive to her house with her husband.

"Nice try. He's heading right over to Mom and Dad's. Stop worrying. You're not in trouble." She smiles at me when I open the passenger door of my Jeep, but I don't buy it. I'm always in trouble, and if Gracie told her I did something, then I'm in double trouble.

Nina fills the silence with idle chit-chat about work and a fundraiser coming up, in addition to her frustration that the alteration shop can't seem to get her bridesmaid dress to fit just right. I have no idea what she's talking about, but at least it's not about Gracie or something I've done wrong.

By the time we pull into her driveway, I know all about everything she could possibly want to talk about, and I'm updated from the last time we spoke. I don't mind because I love my sister, but I really wish she would get to the reason she needed to talk to me. Inside, she pulls out a chair at her kitchen table and motions for me to sit. Here we go. The moment of truth. The lead-up to me getting my rear end chewed out for some random thing I did that annoyed her... or Gracie.

"Listen, I'm about to do something I shouldn't do. I'm betraying Gracie's trust, but only because I think it is what's best for her, and I trust you."

Oh, boy.

"Whatever she said that I did, it wasn't like it seemed. I swear. I haven't done anything on purpose, and whatever it was, it was probably a misunderstanding. All I did was help her with her horses, and then I tried to help with the barn and the porch. I didn't mean to upset her if that's what happened."

Nina arches her eyebrows, and her lips draw into a smirk.

"Practice that on the way here?" she asks.

I let out a breath. "Maybe. You two like to gang up on me."

"This isn't that. This is me trying to help my brother understand my best friend and to help my best friend overcome something that has been a problem for many, many years."

My chest tightens. I can't help but wonder if I should stop her and tell her that anything Gracie told her in confidence should be kept as such, but judging by the way Nina rubs her arms and bites her lip, she's already contemplating it.

She looks up at me, and her eyes are already swimming with tears. "She's like a sister to me, Paul, and there are things you don't know. You know she was adopted." She pauses, so I nod. It's common knowledge, so it can't be the big reveal. "Her adoptive parents are great. You know that, too. You spent time at her house and saw how much they love her, but what you don't know is why her biological parents gave her up. She found when we were younger, and it caused a good deal of trauma."

"Oh," I say, leaning closer. Whatever she says will probably give me more insight into Gracie Gallagher's head than I ever thought possible, and now I understand why it's so hard for Nina to discuss.

"They were addicts and in poverty. Rather than try to overcome those hurdles and make a better home for her, they left her on the front steps of a police station and never came back. In Gracie's mind, that's not a good reason. I agree, but it doesn't help her to deny they *had* a reason, no matter how bad it was. She's never heard from them, not even a birthday card. In high school, she discovered they got clean and had three more children."

I can't help that my jaw clenches at this, and Nina doesn't miss it.

"Yeah, me too. I'm angry when I think about it, but can you imagine how it makes Gracie feel?"

I run a hand over my face and try to clear my mind. "Probably pretty awful."

"She fears abandonment over everything else in life. That time when she was depressed in school... Well, maybe you don't remember, but both times, it was because of that. Then the thing happened with you two at prom, and—"

"Wait, what?" It's the second time prom has been brought up, and I have no idea what I did wrong. She got stood up, and I offered to dance with her because I felt bad. I thought I had done the right thing, but clearly, there was something I had missed.

"Prom? The almost kiss?"

I sit straight and almost choke. "The *what?*"

Nina looks at me like I'm insane, and her eyes go wide as if it's some kind of shock that I'm out of the loop here. "You don't know?" I shake my head. "Paul, she thought there was a moment between you, that you almost kissed her. And that wasn't the first time!"

"What? Nina, I have no idea what you're talking about."

She presses her hands on the table and sighs yet again. "I guess she misunderstood, but that doesn't change the fact that she thought the two of you had several moments. You know, times that she thought you were going to kiss her, then you didn't."

"Okay, but why would she even want me to? Why would it bother her that..." The dawn of realization creeps up on me, and I make eye contact with my sister. She widens her eyes and nods. "She... liked me?"

"Past tense?" she asks, urging me to work through this ridiculously complicated problem.

All this time, years of taunting and teasing, and the woman had liked me... was interested in me as... a boyfriend. Suddenly, every interaction I've ever had with Gracie begins to make sense. And that kiss.

"Paul, she will never admit to you that she has feelings for you. She's in a hard place right now trying to make it on her own and accomplish her dream of running her own stable, and I don't know why she kissed you and refuses to tell you why, but she did. I was mad about it for a while because I don't want either of you getting hurt. Can you understand?"

My brain is trying to catch up with what Nina is saying, but I'm stuck back on the part about Gracie having feelings for me since high school, maybe longer.

"She worries about trusting anyone, and more than anything, she's afraid of losing us. *Both* of us."

"That's silly. She'll never lose you."

"I know that, but it's something she will always doubt. You have to understand how much her parents hurt her. It doesn't matter that the Gallaghers love her. It's that her biological parents forgot about her that hurts."

I swallow and instantly regret everything I ever did to tease Gracie. More than that, I realize that I have an uncontrollable urge to hug her and tell her that no matter what went wrong between us, I'll always be her friend.

"Paul?"

I let out a long exhale and tap my fingers on the table. I'm not sure that I want to have this conversation with my sister, but it seems it's going to happen regardless of my comfort level.

"I didn't know that. I honestly had no idea she felt that way, and I certainly had no idea about her parents."

Nina stands and heads to the refrigerator to get the roast for dinner, giving me a moment to gather my thoughts.

"Well, now that you know, do you mind if I ask how you feel?"

I chuckle. "How do I feel? How would I know? I just found out that she has feelings for me, and I'm supposed to know what to do with that?" I have a good idea that the jealous monkey-head that emerged yesterday is a good indicator that I do have some kind of feeling about Gracie, but how far those feelings go is unclear.

She returns from the kitchen with the roast and some other items in a bag. "Well, you better figure it out soon. She's joining us for dinner at Mom and Dad's."

I leap from the chair. "You invited her to dinner? Are you crazy? There's no way I can act normally in front of her after you told me all of that!" I ruffle my hair and start pacing. "Nina, you're such a pain in my rear end, did you know that? What am I supposed to say to her?"

She shrugs. "I don't know. Ask her on a date."

"I did, and she turned me down." Immediately, I regret informing my sister of that, but it seems she already knew. She grimaces and lowers her gaze to the floor. "She told you."

Nina nods. "Yeah, and she also told me she went inside and cried because she wanted to say yes. Paul, I would never ask you to force feelings for her, but if there is any care in your heart for her at all, I would ask you to consider what it means and whether there could be a future for you. If not, then I can try to dissuade her from her feelings towards you."

"I don't know how I feel, but I promise you that I will be gentle and think about everything you said. I don't want to hurt her either, so you don't have to worry about that."

Nina pats my arm and opens her front door. "I know. That's why I decided to tell you."

The whole drive to our parents' house, Nina is quiet, so I can think. I let prom run through my mind until it's almost mush, but for the life of me, I can't figure out at which point she thought I was about to kiss her. Not once had she ever given me any indication that she *wanted* to be kissed, but back then, I can't say I would have picked up on it even if she had outright asked me to.

Gracie's car—and everyone else's—is in the driveway when we reach my parents' house. My heart picks up and Nina gives me yet another of her looks. This one says she's begging me to be kind, to take care of her best friend's heart, and not to make a fool of her. I nod and get out, then help her carry everything inside. The second my gaze lands on Gracie chatting with Calliope and May, I can't help but smile. She looks up to see who entered, and when her gaze connects with mine, she blushes and looks away.

Nina disappears into the kitchen to help our mother, alerting the other ladies that the conversation is moving. Every other Sunday, the Hollis sisters join us for family dinner after church, but it's rare that Gracie joins. She used to frequently when we were younger, but after college, she didn't attend unless there was a holiday or birthday. Usually, the ladies head into the kitchen to chat and cook while the men discuss sports, then clean up after dinner so the ladies can relax.

Gracie refuses to look at me when she passes me, so I grab her arm. She freezes and looks up at me, but before she can issue whatever scathing comment is on the tip of her tongue, I motion toward the door.

"Go for a walk with me?"

"Why?" she asks, crossing her arms.

"Because I'd like to take a walk with you, that's all. I had some ideas about the barn, and I thought it might be nice to chat."

"Oh. Um, I think they want me to help them cook, so—"

"No, go for a walk!" Nina shouts from the kitchen.

Gracie tenses, but I ignore it and lead her toward the door. It's shut behind us before she can utter another comment, and I'm already down the front stairs. She has no choice but to go with me, or hide out somewhere to avoid Nina's pestering.

"Well, what are your ideas?" she asks, her arms crossed again as she heads toward the sidewalk. I walk alongside her, wracking my brain for ideas because I told her a little fib. I have zero plans for the barn, but it was the only thing I could think of to get her to go for a walk with me. She looks up at me expectantly, but all I can see is the hope in her eyes. She doesn't even know it's there, most likely, but I see the way she looks at me now. It's always with hope, with some prayer that I will *see* her and not just look at her. I didn't know that was what it meant back then. Well, I see her now, and I can't stop looking.

"Um, I was thinking of a different design. Maybe Edwin can help us with that. Something that might last longer."

"I sort of figured we'd build something sturdier, but asking Edwin is a good idea."

She starts walking again, and we end up in front of old man Peterson's house, the one with a tall fence and so many vines from the fence to the trees on the other sidewalk, it creates a sort of tunnel over the walkway. Under it, hidden from anyone driving by or anyone spying on us from their homes, I pause and grasp her elbow. I pull her slightly, and she scowls when she turns around to face me.

"What?" she snaps.

"Why do you do that to me? Why do you snap at me when I'm trying to be nice to you?" I run my hand over her elbow and up her arm to her shoulder. She doesn't shirk it, but she's stiff as a board.

She flinches. "I'm sorry. I'm stressed, but you're right. I shouldn't have snapped at you."

Her apology surprises me, but not enough to deter me from our conversation. "Gracie," I whisper, careful not to scare her away. She's flighty, already nervous, and her eyes dart back and forth, everywhere but on me. "Gracie, look at me."

She stares at her feet.

"You don't care for following directions, do you?"

"Why did we stop here, Paul?"

"Because I have a question."

She sighs so hard it makes her cheeks puff. "I told you that I'd talk about the kiss with you when I'm ready." She frowns and shakes her head. "It was stupid. It was a practical joke that went sideways, that's all. It didn't mean anything. Can we just move on and forget it happened?"

"That wasn't what my question was going to be, but I don't think that's the truth. Why did you kiss me in the parking lot, Gracie? Tell me the truth, please." I step forward and run my other hand up her other arm, forcing chills to rise over her skin. With both hands on her shoulders, I step closer, trail my fingers up the back of her neck, and tilt her head back.

"Just let it go. Forget it happened. It meant nothing." She shivers again but doesn't move away.

"What if I don't want to forget it, Gracie?"

She shakes her head slightly, but she doesn't break eye contact. "Paul," she warns.

"I don't want to forget about it. I haven't been able to *stop* thinking about it since it happened. Please don't lie to me. If it truly meant nothing to you, tell me now before I kiss you again."

"Wh... what?" Her breathy reply settles on my ears like a flutter, and I'm beginning to know what my feelings are. The jealousy over Christian, the disappointment when she declined my dinner offer, the way my heart pounds just holding her this way. Her blue eyes question me with each blink. Each breath.

"Gracie, tell me what to do." I lean my forehead on hers, wishing I could just kiss her. I want to kiss her and hold her and eliminate every fear she has that I might abandon her. I won't. I can't because my prayer from church comes back to me. If Nina pulling me aside and telling me her best friend has feelings for me isn't a sign, I don't know what is.

"Paul... I... I can't." She jerks away from me and rushes from beneath the tunnel.

"Gracie, wait!" I follow after her but make no move to stop her. "Gracie, I'm sorry. I didn't mean to—"

"No. It isn't... it isn't you." She spins around. "It's me. It's always me, and I can't have this conversation with you. I just can't, Paul. So please, forget about the kiss, forget about what it did or didn't mean, and just... just let me live my life."

With that, she marches back to my parents' house. If she thinks that's all it takes to dismiss me, she's got another thought coming.

Chapter Seven
Gracie

CHAPTER SEVEN

Gracie

His footsteps tap behind me. All I have to do is turn around and admit that I lied, that the kiss meant everything to me, even if it meant nothing to him, but I can't. Opening up that much to him will kill me, especially if this is only an experiment for him. He only wants to kiss me again because he's intrigued, not because there are any real feelings between us.

"Gracie," he pleads, so I walk faster. He jogs around in front of me. "Gracie, please."

I halt, not because I want to but because the tone of his voice is nothing like I've ever heard before. Pleading is not common for Paul, so the way his voice is strained and hurt gives me pause. It's just enough time for him to put his hands up defensively and slip inside of my mind, around that wall that I've made extra thick.

"May I please speak, and then you can do whatever you want?"

I nod and cross my arms over my torso, protecting myself from whatever he is about to say.

"I think you lied to me, but it's okay. I only want you to know three things, things to think about before you write this off and run away. First, if the kiss really meant nothing and it was a joke, I still want us to stop the bickering and be friends. I care about you, and I enjoyed the time we've spent together the past two days. Second, if it *did* mean something to you, but you've changed your mind about it, that is okay, too. I still want to be friends. Third, if it did mean something, and it still does, but you're too afraid to admit it..." He pauses to take a breath, almost as if what he's about to say scares the life out of him. "If it did mean something, and you're afraid, that's alright. I want you to know that after spending a lot of time thinking about it, that it meant something to me."

My heart aches. What did it mean to him, exactly? I should ask, but fear cinches my throat closed so no sound can come out. All I can do is stare at the sidewalk in front of me, scared like the kid I was every single time I thought there was a moment between us in the past. Every time I wanted to tell him that our bantering hurt me because I cared for him in ways I shouldn't care about my best friend's brother.

"Can I ask you another question? The one I intended to ask you earlier?" His tone is lighter now, which makes me involuntarily lift my head to look at him. "Why was there a duck in the library?"

I burst out into laughter and the tension between us is immediately gone. Paul nudges my shoulder with his, turning me around back the way we were headed when we began our walk. I go with him because it seems as though he's changing the subject on purpose, giving me the out I desperately need if I am going to survive this dinner. And I want to. I want to get to know Calliope and May since Nina loves them so much. I want to keep fitting in with this family. I need them.

"Seriously, I need to know why there was a duck. It's been bugging me."

I can't help laughing again as we walk side-by-side down the sidewalk. "It lives in the pond out front, and someone left the front door open. That day was a catastrophe. Shelby found boogers in a book."

Paul pauses and glances at me before erupting in laughter. "Like real boogers in a book or a book about boogers?"

"Like a kid used the book to wipe his boogers on. It was disgusting. There was jelly on everything, and the busted pipe took forever to clean up. The bathroom is still out of order, so we have to walk next door to the gas station to use the restroom there. I don't need to tell you how gross a gas station restroom is."

"Sounds like a crummy day. I'm sorry I made it worse," he says but doesn't linger on it, almost as if he knows what it will do if he stays on the topic for too long. "Did you know we have a distant relative who died on the USS Arizona?"

"I did not. That explains your obsession with the organization of the World War II exhibit. I do know the order of events, by the way. People just don't put things back where they belong."

"Well, that isn't the only reason I like history. There's so much to learn and so little time. I learn something new every day, and I think it's one of the least appreciated subjects in school. I don't understand why, though. The answers literally are written down, and all you have to do is remember."

"Literature is a good subject, too." I spy his grimace from the corner of my eye. "Yeah, I know. You hated it, but if you had asked me nicely, I would have tutored you."

"You terrified me, to be honest. You're so smart, and it always seemed like you knew exactly what you wanted and where you were going in life. I kind of admired it, actually. Still do."

I lick my lips and try to keep up the conversation. It's nice, but I'm getting nervous. We're getting very close to those things I don't want to discuss, especially school. It was not a good time, and the only reason I was so focused was because it dulled the pain and gave me something to concentrate on besides my imploding life. Paul brushes his fingers over my elbow.

"We can talk about something else, like... Oh, did you know that Calliope is an author?"

"Nina mentioned it, yes. I'm not sure I'd like her style of writing, but it is nice to have someone in the family who has the same interests as me." I immediately realize what I said, that I am not actually a part of their family, and I cringe. "I meant to say, it's nice that... I mean, I know I'm not your family, but... you know what I mean."

"You are part of the family, Gracie. You always have been." Paul shrugs as if this is common knowledge, and I'm silly if I thought otherwise. It's oddly comforting, so I go with it and don't fight him on the matter.

My shoulders relax, and that stone in my gut eases. This is nice. I can do this. Just walk and talk with Paul like it's something we've always done. My mind drifts back to what he said—that the kiss meant something to him—and I wonder if I should admit that it meant something to me, too. The stone rolls back in, so I decide it's probably not a good idea to admit that, not yet... maybe never. There is every chance in the world that after a time dating, Paul would decide I'm not right for him and leave me. If my parents could do it, then so could he. After all, parents are supposed to love you more than anyone else in the world, so it stands to reason that Paul's commitment to me would falter in time. I try not to think the same of Nina. It's like swallowing a thorn.

"So, like I said yesterday, Christian said he could finish the demo of the barn on his own, but if you want a little help with the other repairs around the house, I don't mind helping out. With Callie and May in the picture, the guys are busier. I get bored."

I bite the instinct to snap at him in a misguided attempt to stay independent and nod. "That would be nice, actually. I have everything I need to get the roof fixed but haven't been able to hire anyone to do it."

Paul nudges me with his shoulder again and says, "I happen to be an expert roofer."

"Paul, you fell off your grandmother's roof twice three summers ago," I say with an eye roll.

"Right, so I know exactly what *not* to do."

"You broke your arm! Maybe that's not the right job to ask you to do. Let's stick to things that keep your feet on the ground," I tease.

"Well, what else is there?"

I think about all of the things that need to be done at home, and that leads me to think about Paul doing all of those things for me. Having him at my house that much could spell trouble, but if I don't accept his help, I might never get anything done. It's a conundrum, and I hate it. I suppose I'm quiet for too long, so he brushes his fingers over my arm again.

"I'm being pushy. I'm sorry. You tell me if you need something, and I'll be there. If not, that's fine."

"Thank you," I whisper. I have never seen this side of him before, and frankly, it's intimidating. Having his full attention was all I wanted way back when, but I had no idea how actually having it might feel. Good. It feels amazing, but it also feels like it might kill me if I let it become something I depend on, only to lose it.

"The ponies and your horses are getting along well, May said." He's changed the subject again.

"Yeah. Her ponies are so cute. I've never seen John so smitten before, and to quit his job?" I look up at Paul to see his reaction. It's true. Edwin and John are so happy, and I can't remember a time I've ever seen them so elated about anything. Of course, Edwin is still particular, but he's also dependable. John is still intimidating but also loyal. It's at this moment that I realize how devastated I would be to lose anyone in this family.

My chest pinches, and it's hard to breathe. I don't realize I've stopped walking until Paul turns and faces me.

"Gracie?"

"I... I can't... breathe." Huffs of breath wheeze out between words.

"What's wrong?" Paul grasps my upper arms and peers down at me.

I shake my head and try to pull away, eyes darting everywhere. What if I lose all of them? If Nina ever gets upset with me, then they will all go away. They're a family and a close one. If one hates me, then they would all hate me. They would all leave and never speak to me again. I try to breathe again, but my throat is too tight. My lungs burn. My skin tingles, and my head feels light. Suddenly, it's like I'm watching everything from outside, like looking into a snow globe, part of it but on the outside. It doesn't seem real, and darkness rims the edges of my vision.

"Gracie, sit down. Come here." Paul guides me to a bench just ahead, but I stumble over my own feet. He helps me sit, but the world is swirling in colors so bright I can't think.

"Tell me five things you see, Gracie."

"What?" I snap.

"Just tell me five things you see. Focus on five things and tell me what you see."

I shut my eyes tightly for a moment, then open them and try to pick out things. I have no idea what I'm doing or why, but I finally focus on a stop sign. "A stop sign."

"Okay. Four more things."

"Trees," I huff. "Roses. A person walking a dog. Grass."

"Tell me four things you hear."

"Paul, I can't—"

"Four things you hear, Gracie. It's okay. Trust me," Paul urges.

"Birds. The dog barked. Traffic. Um... people talking down the street."

"Three things you smell."

I don't fight him this time. I inhale deeply and try to pick up on the subtle scents all around. "The roses behind us. Someone is baking bread. Maybe it's the bakery the next street over. Um..." What else do I smell? This is such a weird thing to do. "Um... cut grass."

"Okay, tell me two things you feel."

I focus on what I feel, my sense of touch. "My jeans against my hand." I realize he's holding my other hand, gently stroking the back of it with his thumb. It makes me weak, but I'm focused. Everything feels normal again. "You."

"What's one thing you can taste?" he asks.

I turn my head and focus on him. "Taste?" I chuckle, and he laughs.

"Well, you're grounded now, aren't you?" He scoots forward on the bench and shifts to face me better. "You had a panic attack. Has that ever happened before?"

I swallow hard. Yep. But this is the first time anyone ever cared enough to help me through it. And he *did* help me immensely. "It used to happen a lot in high school, but this is the first time I got over it that fast. Thank you."

"Not a problem. They teach us that in college. It's a grounding technique that helps kids feel safer when everything seems like it's spinning out of control."

Ugh... he's going to ask me what caused it. Please don't ask... please don't ask...

"Do you want to talk about what happened? Did I do something?"

"No, and no," I say, but I squeeze his hand before I stand. "I'd like to head back now if that's okay. I'm getting hungry after that exercise."

Paul chuckles and joins me. He lets the whole thing go without another word or another question, and for that, I am grateful. Not even Nina would let me get away without expounding on the root cause of my panic. I want to tell him that, let him know that what he did really helped me. I don't know if it will matter to him, so I keep quiet instead.

We walk in blessed silence most of the way back, but before we turn into the driveway, he pauses. Fudge pops. He's going to ask me something I don't want to answer. And if I don't, he might get annoyed. The best way to avoid this is to say something first.

"I'm starving. Your mom's roast is always the best."

"Yeah," he says, but he's not easily deterred. "Gracie?"

I clench my jaw and hum. "Hmm?"

"I'm not going anywhere. Not now, and not later." He leans over and kisses my cheek, then jogs up the stairs to open the door for me.

Chapter Eight
Paul

"I SAID, FIGURE OUT your feelings, not cause a panic attack!" Nina fusses at me in the back room of our parents' house. Right after dinner, she pulled me aside and gave me her best scowl.

"What did Gracie say happened?" I ask, which seems like the logical thing to ask since I thought I had done everything right. Gracie hadn't seemed upset or angry with me after the fact, but who knows what she might have told Nina.

"She didn't say anything, but I know her. She has post-panic attack vibes." Nina rolls her eyes.

"Vibes? So, you're assuming I did something wrong, and that triggered Gracie's panic attack?" Annoyance bubbles up, and I'm three seconds from telling my sister, who means well, to mind her own business.

"She hasn't had one in a long time, and I'm just worried about her, okay?"

I sigh and run my hand through my hair to keep from saying things I shouldn't. Instead, I try to remember that Nina truly does have Gracie's best interests at heart. "She did have an attack, but I talked her down from it, and when we parted, she was fine. Did it ever occur to you that constantly treating a grown woman with kid gloves might not be the best way to help her?"

"Don't act like you suddenly know her better than I do," she snaps, then leaves me standing in the room alone. I cannot win for losing with these two, and I think that might be the problem. Things between Gracie and me cannot possibly be sorted and figured out if we have someone in the middle dictating our shots. As much as I love and adore my sister, she's gotta get out of our way.

Telling her that is the problem.

"No, she did not!" Gracie squeals at Edwin's retelling of the pepper spray incident, and it makes me smile. She seems fine now, with no lingering stress from the attack. I have no idea what Nina's picking up on, but there's a small part of me that wonders if Nina needs Gracie to need her more than Gracie actually needs her. I don't open that box because it's more psychological mumbo jumbo than I am equipped to handle. I shiver just thinking about the complications of a woman needing to belong and another woman needing her to need to belong, all while the first one needs to be needed by me, and the second needing me to need her to need me. It's a lot of need, and my brain feels like overworked bread by the time I make it back to the living room.

Rhodes offers me a sympathetic gaze, but he knows if he even touches this situation with a ten-foot pole, he'll only be as confused as I am.

Gracie glances up at me and smiles, then gives her attention back to Edwin. Calliope's face is bright red, but she takes our family ribbing like a sport.

"I'm never going to live that down," Calliope says. "Someone else have a turn."

"What are we playing?" I ask. I sit beside John because it seems a lot safer than sitting beside Nina or Gracie, and there's not a chance I'm sitting beside the lovely but disastrous Calliope. I have enough trouble without adding a broken nose or some other disaster to it.

"Sharing our most embarrassing moments," Rhodes says.

"It was hard for Callie, but I think I have to agree that was a pretty embarrassing one. Now it's Gracie's turn," May says, tucking her blonde hair behind her before giving Gracie all of her attention. Chances are, sweet May has no idea how self-conscious Gracie is. She wouldn't know that most of her embarrassing moments probably happened in my presence, and when Gracie's eyes flash with panic, I can't help but step in.

"I know what her most embarrassing moment was," I say, earning a death glare from both Gracie and Nina. Honestly, it feels like they think I'm an idiot, but I know what I'm doing... sometimes. "It was back in middle school when we had soccer practice. You kicked the ball so hard it knocked Joey Conner out cold. He didn't live that down for a year."

Gracie's eyes go wide. "I forgot all about that!"

Everyone starts laughing, and while it wasn't exactly embarrassing at all—in fact, most people thought it was pretty awesome—it saved her from admitting what embarrassed her most... me. John and Edwin dive into the logistics and physics involved with such a feat while the ladies regale their own sports injuries to one another. Gracie, though, makes eye contact with me.

Her soft smile melts me. "Thank you," she mouths, then looks away and rejoins the conversation.

An hour after dinner, my father gets the grand idea that we should play a round of flag football in the backyard. This is all fine and good, except I know his idea of flag football usually means someone gets injured and ends up in the hospital. This seems like a horrible idea since Calliope, the undefeated champion of pain-inducing incidents, is now part of the family fun. Still, he charges on like he hasn't heard every single one of May and Edwin's stories about our girl.

"Alright, on my team—"

"Oh, no," Mom says. "You don't choose first. You always choose first, and you always choose John. I go first this time, and my eldest son is on his mama's team. Deal with it."

Dad chuckles but concedes. "Fine, fine. John is on his mommy's team."

"You're not funny, Dad," John says but kisses May's cheek and jogs to join our mother.

The teams continue to divide. Nina backs out because she's still wearing a dress, so now we're uneven. Rhodes decides he'll sit out this round and fill in when there's an injury. Fair enough, but I'm somewhat freaked out that Calliope is on my team along with Mom and John. But then, having her on the opposing team might be just as bad.

We begin the game, and I don't miss Gracie's death stare. I can't tell if she's actually mad at me or if she's just trying to intimidate me. The second thought makes me chuckle a little, so I'm not paying the least bit of attention to my teammates. Bad idea. John launches like a racehorse with the ball, dodges Edwin and May, then hurtles toward our made-up end zone. I finally realize he's trying to get my attention and put my hands up to catch the ball he has hurdled a thousand miles an hour right at my face. Only Calliope is small, and I don't notice her behind me when I step back, so I stumble. She goes down, trips me, and the ball smashes into my face so hard little birdies sing all around me.

"Oomph, you're heavy. Get off! Get off!" Calliope shouts beneath me, but the wind was knocked out of me, so I can't breathe, let alone move. John shoves me aside and rescues our mini-teammate, leaving me to fend for myself. Once I catch my breath, I sit up and look for Calliope. She's scowling at me.

"I said I got it like a hundred times." Her little fists on her hips are funny, so I chuckle and offer my hand.

"Spectacular fail," I say, and she gives me a high five along with an eye roll.

"Nice catch," Gracie teases.

"Okay, smarty pants. Your time is coming."

"It's flag football, Paul. Not tackle, so don't even think about pulling a seventh-grade again." She glares at me, a warning, but I don't remember seventh grade, so I don't worry. I'm gonna do what I want anyway.

Once again, she's got me distracted, but it's okay. Somehow, May gets the ball and takes off like she's going to make it if she just moves those little feet fast enough. Not a chance with her future husband on my team. John reaches her, and, rather than yank the flag free, he catches her around the waist and literally tosses her at me—the whole woman flies through the air. Naturally, I catch her and run like wild the opposite way, scoring a touchdown... I think.

Nina decides scoring while carrying a woman holding the ball is acceptable. Rhodes seconds her decision, so we're up by one. May throws the ball and hits me in the head.

"Hey, don't be a sore loser!" I shout.

A bony finger pokes me in the ribs, eliciting a girlish squeal I am not proud of. "Don't pick on my teammate," Gracie says, then jogs over to join May in their planning. Dad shakes his head at me and joins the ladies and Edwin.

"What's going on between you and Gracie?" Mom steps beside me, panting, although she hasn't done anything but run up and down the yard, yelling at us to hurry up.

"What do you mean? Nothing is going on."

She snorts. "Okay."

"Alright, this time we won't be taken down so easily," Dad insists, earning a chuckle from John.

"We'll see," John says, rubbing his hands together.

Edwin arches an eyebrow and meets him head-to-head. "Don't underestimate me or my ability to distract my fiancé."

Oh, no. This is about to require ice and an ambulance. I know it.

I catch the ball and bullet before Calliope can get anywhere near it. If I stay ahead of my teammate, then I can't trip over her. Mom shouts at me to run faster, but I'm already going as fast as my feet can take me—then I hurdle forward and smash my face into the dirt. The air rushes from my lungs again, and I wheeze it back in just as Gracie rolls me over and puts her knee on my chest.

"*That* was for seventh grade," she says, grabs the ball, and disappears.

The clouds overhead drift by while I count the seconds it takes for my spleen to stop hurting. John appears in my line of sight, standing over me.

"Are you alright? You went down like a sack of potatoes."

"I'm in pain," I groan.

He offers his hand and pulls me up, smacks me on the back, and says, "That's what you get for tackling her all those years ago."

"You remember?"

"How can you not? She had to go to the ortho-surgeon."

"Huh?" I try to brush the dirt from my shirt, but it's ground in too deep.

"The ortho... are you kidding me? You knocked out two of her teeth!" John shakes his head and jogs back over to May. Evidently, Gracie scored, and the game is over. No one cares that we are tied. They only want my mother's apple pie, so they're filing inside. I ruffle grass from my hair and head that way, but Gracie grabs my hand and tugs me back. I have no clue she was even behind me because I'm still a little dazed after eating mud.

"Hey, sorry I hit you so hard. That was kind of jerky." Her cheeks blaze red, but I know she means it.

"Fair is fair. Sorry that I knocked your teeth out."

"You don't even remember." She frowns, and it hits me hard. I don't remember, but it's not because she wasn't someone I cared about.

"I'm sorry that I don't. It's not because I don't care. I just—"

"I know." She interrupts me and shrugs. "You can recite facts and figures from history like an encyclopedia. You remember a lot of things most people don't even know. Battles, voyages, and things like that are fun for you to explore. It's just how your brain works."

Maybe so, but it's not fair to her. It's not a good excuse to forget all of the things that happened between us. History... *our* history, and I've forgotten most of it. Still, I think I can explain why, so I go for it.

"I was so shy back then. It didn't seem like it, but I was always freaking out on the inside about what people thought about me. It occupied a lot of my time, but I always knew what you thought. I guess I never worried about you because I knew you'd always be here, right with Nina, and there was something sort of comforting in that."

She stands straighter and tilts her head just a little. She's trying to figure me out, but I'm not even sure if I can figure myself out most of the time. All I know is I don't want her to think she meant nothing—*means* nothing—to me.

"Um, so after work tomorrow, I need to ride a few of the horses. Would you... I mean, if you think... Um..." She averts her gaze and struggles a bit more before saying, "Never mind." She tucks the ball under her arm and heads toward the house to get a slice of pie, I assume, but there is zero chance I'm letting her get away that easily.

"Hey," I shout. She turns, her cheeks bright red. "I'd love to go riding with you tomorrow afternoon. Then I'd also like to take you to dinner."

Gracie bites her lip and glances away, then nods. "Yeah. Okay."

Chapter Nine
Gracie

It's been a slow day, which is good since the plumber is fixing the toilet, and we still have to go through the entire catalog to see what books need to be replaced. Shelby sighs for the tenth time as she scrolls and cross-checks everything. It's not the most fun part of our jobs, and we've both dreamed about different getting new ones multiple times today.

"So, what did you do this weekend?" Shelby asks. She's already asked three times, and every single time, I have changed the subject.

"Not much. Tore down the barn so it can be fixed. Had dinner at Nina's on Sunday."

Shelby lifts her head and arches an eyebrow. "And was that delicious snack there as well?"

"Ew, shut up." I throw my notepad at her.

"You're violent when it comes to that man. Did you know that?" She hands me back the pad and stands to stretch. She checks her watch and gasps. "Oh, wow. It's closing time, my friend."

"Really?" I check my watch and, sure enough, we have three minutes left. The plumber is packing up, and it looks like we have a brand-new toilet. My nerves start to get the better of me thinking about the upcoming date with Paul. No, not a date. It's two friends hanging out, going on a horseback ride, then dinner. I've done that with Nina many times.

Shelby shuts down all of the computers and checks the rooms for stragglers. Everyone left hours ago, so all that's left to do is turn off the lights and lock up. The sky looks nasty, and disappointment sets in. If we get an afternoon storm, then we won't be able to go riding, which means less time spent with Paul. It's probably a sign.

"See you tomorrow, sunshine. I want to get out of here before it opens up on us." Shelby waves over her shoulder and darts towards her car just as the first sound of thunder rolls in. Perfect. If I had known it was going to storm, I wouldn't have stuttered my way through asking Paul to join me. Not that I did ask him. He figured it out and invited himself, which is equally as embarrassing as asking him myself.

I slide into my driver's seat and slam the door, frustrated. I shove the key in the ignition and turn, but... nothing. I try again and again, but there is zero life in my car. I let my head fall on the steering wheel, blaring the horn. After a dramatic moment or two, I pull my phone from my bag. I don't even know who to call. My parents are on *another* cruise, and Nina is still at work. I don't want to pull her away from it, especially when she's so busy getting a fundraiser organized. I bite my lip as one other name comes to mind. School has been out for two hours, and it's just around the corner. There's a good chance Paul hasn't left yet, so I give in and call him.

He doesn't answer after three rings, and I'm about to give up hope when he finally answers.

"Hey, what's up?" he asks, sounding winded.

"Uh, if you're busy—"

"I'm not. I just finished playing basketball with the team. I was about to shower before meeting you."

"Well, it's storming, so it doesn't look like we'll get to ride today, but I also have a problem. My car won't start. I'm stuck at work."

"Are you safe? Can I spare ten minutes to shower, and I'll come get you?"

"Yeah, of course. I'll just go back into the library and wait. Thanks."

"Sure, make sure to lock up behind you. I'll hurry."

"Yep," I say, then hang up because I never know how to get off the phone with anyone. It's always awkward with the goodbyes and see you laters. Between thunder cracks, I bolt to the library and get back inside, then lock the doors behind me. At least there are books to read while I wait, but I'm still upset I won't get to go riding. I miss my babies, and riding always puts my nerves at ease. I need a good, relaxing ride.

I browse the romance novels for a bit, scoffing at all of the ridiculous blurbs. There is nothing in any of those books that is even remotely like real life, which I am reminded of every time I think about my own love life... or lack of it. Sure, I've gone on dates, but no one ever compares to... the guy pounding on the door getting soaked.

"Paul!" I shout and run to the door to let him in. He hurries in and shuts the door behind him. "I figured you'd call me when you arrived!"

"It got kinda crazy out there. I thought it would be safer inside until it dies down a bit." He peers out the window up at the sky. "It's seriously nasty. Sorry about the horseback riding. I was looking forward to it."

I stuff my hands in my pockets because I don't know what else to do with them when he looks at me the way he is, as if he's waiting for some response that will give him insight into my brain. "Yeah, me too. It is what it is."

"Maybe tomorrow?"

"Oh, uh, I guess that could work." Duh, that thought never occurred to me.

"What do you have to do around here while we wait for the storm to pass? I'm not crazy about lifting the hood of your car and fidgeting with things in the middle of a parking lot during a thunderstorm." He grins and nods over his shoulder.

"We have books," I say flatly enough that it makes him chuckle.

"So you do." Paul shirks his coat and ruffles the water from his hair before wandering the aisles. I'm not sure if I'm supposed to follow him or not, so I stay put and watch him. His eyes dart with wonder as he browses the history section and, every so often, pulls a gem from the shelf. He's truly in love with history, and it's kind of adorable in a sweet, boyish way. He drags his eyes away from one of the books and looks up at me. "Come here. I want to show you something."

It's a book about the USS Arizona, and he positions himself to show me what he's reading. I lean over to read it, but I'm not so sure I know why I'm reading it.

"That's my distant relative I was telling you about. I know it's silly, but reading about this makes me feel closer to him in a way, like I get a glimpse of what it was like back then." He blushes and pulls the book back. "It's weird. I know."

Crazy Gracie enters the picture, and I tug him closer, book and all. "I don't think that's crazy. It's sweet, actually. We are made of memories, and if we forget our history, then we're not only doomed to repeat it, but look like a bunch of idiots when we do. History is important, and I don't think you're silly or weird for liking it."

Paul stares down at me with soft eyes and a small smile. "I forgot our history for a while. I'm sorry for that."

I want to say something, tell him it's okay as long as we don't repeat it, but lighting flashes, and at the same time, thunder crashes so loudly it rumbles through my body. The power blinks out, and I scream. In the process, Paul grabs me to steady me, and I fall into him, knocking him backward. His back smashes against the bookshelf, knocking half the case over. Books sail across the room and scatter all over the floor. I press my palms against his chest to right myself while he grips my elbows. His heart is racing as fast as mine, so I laugh and stand upright.

"Your heart is racing. That scared me, too. Too bad we don't have a backup generator. I think there's a flashlight under the desk, though. Gimme a sec."

Paul grasps my wrist and pulls me back. "It wasn't the power going out that's got my heart racing, Gracie. It's you."

Oh.

"Please say I can kiss you now." He presses his forehead to mine the same way he did yesterday, and it takes every single ounce of my willpower to resist him. He smells like soap and rain and books, and I want to kiss him so badly my entire body is weak, but I can't. It'll only bring on so much regret later when things don't work out.

"Paul, I... I don't think that's a good idea."

A huff of breath escapes his lips, and he releases me. Warm, comforting eyes stare down at me, and he smiles. It's fake, but it's also for my benefit, and I want to cry. He's offering me the exact thing I've wanted for so, so long, and I turn him down? What kind of idiot am I? Probably the kind who forgets history and repeats everything she ever did wrong, but I don't care. I might live to regret this, but right now, I'm going to give in. I'm going to enjoy the thing I've always wanted, and if it blows up in my face later, then so be it.

I push up on my toes, ready to kiss him like I did in the parking lot, but he dodges me. Humiliation and regret slam into me like a freight train, and my cheeks catch on fire. I shove away from him and turn my back, rush past the desk, and head for the bathroom. I can lock myself in until the storm is over, then beg Nina to pick me up and take me home, where I can bury my face in pillows and pretend that did not just happen.

"Gracie Gallagher, get your cute butt back here right now." Paul grasps my elbow and spins me around. This seems to have become a habit, and I'm ready to give him a good scolding when he covers my lips with a finger. "You said no, and I respected your answer. I don't want to be kissed because you suddenly feel vulnerable or guilty. *Stop* getting mad and storming away from me, please."

I scowl, which is hard to do when he's got his finger on my lips. All I want to do is run away, and he's in the way.

"If I release you, are you going to talk to me or hit me?"

I narrow my eyes, and he drops his hand. "Neither."

"Where does that leave us?" His blonde hair is soaked, and all I can think about is running my hands through it. Am I vulnerable? Yes. I'm always a hot mess on the verge of a breakdown, but I'm definitely not feeling guilty. I can't be guilted into kissing anyone, but I still can't decide if this is a good idea. It's probably not, and I'm definitely going to regret it in the morning. I'll also regret it if I don't, so if I have to live with the feeling either way, I might as well charge full steam ahead into the unknown and take Paul Loughton with me.

I step forward, which is all the prompting he needs.

Then it's like I've been sucked into an alternate reality. The kiss in the parking lot was great, and I've thought about it literally every single day, wishing it had been something we had both wanted. And even though he kissed me back that day, it was different. It was shock and intrigue, but this... this is not that at all. When Paul intends to kiss a woman, there is no mistaking that she is his target.

His hair isn't as wet as I thought, but tangling my fingers in it is as wonderful as I had expected. He presses his lips harder and pulls me closer, ignoring the crashing outside. In the library, we're in a different world. One where this can work, and he's actually kissing me because we belong together, we're right. Paul backs me against the check-out counter, and I trip backward, breaking the kiss for a moment. He lifts me and puts me on it, relieving the height difference between us, then kisses me again in less than a breath. The pencil holder ends up on the floor, along with a stack of coloring pages. I don't care. I just want Paul and this all-consuming need to be needed by him, to be wanted not just for a little while but always.

And my brain kicks in.

Paul releases me long enough to trail kisses from my chin to my ear, to whisper softly that he's not going anywhere, and I want to believe him. I want to believe that this is it, the piece of my life that finally works out... but I can't.

My body tenses against my will, and Paul stops kissing me. He pulls back, gaze questioning me. I can't look at him, not now, not after showing that much of myself to him. He knows these kisses mean something, that they mean *everything*, and it's too much. I'm too open, too exposed, and I spiral again.

"Hey, look at me," he says, grasping my chin. I try but end up looking at his chest instead. "Gracie, you're safe with me, I promise you." He backs away and takes a breath. "The storm's settling. I'll check your car while you... uh... I'll just... I'll give you a minute, but you don't have to worry, Gracie."

"Okay," I whisper. "I'll just clean up a little." I slide from the counter and head to pick up the books. I don't know what happened. No, I do, but I don't want to admit that I'm the reason this won't work out. It has nothing to do with him and everything to do with my inability to just let it go, let go of what was done to me, and rise above it. The front door closes, and I take a few deep breaths.

Through the window, I see Paul stop in front of my car. He runs his hands over his face and stares up at the dark sky. He says something, but I don't hear it, then he closes his eyes. I realize he's praying, and while I can't make out every word, I know my name when I see it slip from his lips. My whole body tingles, and I wonder if this is the first time I've been in his prayers.

I manage to peel my eyes off him and get to work cleaning up the mess we made. The mess I made, is more correct. And boy, is it a big mess. I'm not sure how I will ever turn this around, but I know I have to. God has put the thing I've asked for right in front of me, and I'm screwing it up left and right, so I put my mind to my work. Once the books are shelved, the desk is arranged, and my emotions are in check, I head outside with a commitment in mind. I'm going to let him show me all the things he needs me to see, let him lead me and my heart, and pray that giving in is what God wants me to do.

Chapter Ten
Paul

"DON'T TURN AROUND. JUST listen."

I've got my head under the hood of her car when Gracie approaches from behind and issues my order like a drill instructor. I cannot think about anything else but that kiss and how I want to kiss her for the rest of my life, so following instructions is difficult at the moment. The battery is shot, and no amount of jumping it will work. I'm done under the hood, but I want to hear what she's got to say, so I tinker a little more.

"Yes, the kiss in the feed store parking lot meant something to me. I don't know what came over me, but it meant a lot to me. The kiss just now meant even more, but I'm beyond terrified of the future. My past is riddled with people who don't want me, and that makes it pretty hard to see a future that's somehow different. I've wanted your attention since long before the swimming pool incident, and I cover those feelings with hostility and abrasiveness to protect my heart." She pauses, so I think maybe I'm supposed to say something or turn around. I stand straight, and her sharp intake of breath says that was not the right move. I lean forward again, resting my hands on the front of the car.

"I'm almost done. It's just that I realized a little bit ago that maybe that's not fair to you. Maybe this need to protect myself causes you harm, and that's the last thing I want to do. I don't want to push you away or argue with you anymore, but I hope you understand that I don't know where that leaves us. I'm too afraid to move forward but too embarrassed to keep doing the same thing on repeat."

She's quiet again, but I wait. This is not news to me, but the fact that she's standing here telling me means more than those kisses.

"Are you going to say anything?" she asks.

I chuckle. "I didn't know if I was allowed." I start to turn around, and she backs up. "Gracie, come here. Don't run away."

"I don't want to." Her eyes swim with tears, so I concede and turn around again. I feel silly talking to the underside of a car, but if it's what she needs to avoid flight, then I'll do it.

"Do you want to tell me about these things in the past?" I tense. Please, let her say yes.

"I do, but you'll probably think I'm overreacting."

I don't dare tell her that I know. I hate lying, but with so much trust on the line, I can't throw my sister under the bus like that. Besides, letting Gracie tell me in her own way, in her own time, is probably better.

"I want to hear, and I will not think you are overreacting. How do you feel about me taking you home and we can talk on the way? Or we can go to my house, and I'll make you dinner."

Shivers shoot down my spine when she runs her hand over my shoulder, down my back, and settles it on my waist. I stand straight and turn halfway to wrap my arm around her shoulders.

"Car battery is shot. We can't do anything about it right now, so let me take care of you, and we can talk about it, okay?" All those unshed tears break my heart, but this is good. At least, I think it's good.

"I don't think I've ever had your cooking. Is it any good?" she teases, trying to smile through her sorrow.

"It's decent enough to keep me alive, but if you're expecting something as good as my mother's food, you're out of luck." I slam the hood closed and offer my hand. To my surprise, she takes it. She is not going to make this easy, and I'm probably going to want to smash my head into a wall more than once, but I know she's worth it. I've seen her laughter and her good heart. I've seen her ups as well as her downs, and I can handle them both.

In my Jeep, she rubs her arms, so I hand her my coat. She slips her arms through the sleeves and inhales. I try not to be too obvious about the fact that her inhaling my scent is sort of an ego boost by looking out the side window. There's another storm rolling in, or maybe this is only a break in one massive one, so I get moving while I can.

Gracie doesn't say much but hums along to the faint music playing all the way to my townhouse. I have absolutely no idea what I'm going to cook for her, but I'm not so sure it matters. I have a feeling the meal is merely a technicality, something she agreed to, so she'll be distracted enough to talk.

Thank goodness my home is clean. It isn't like I entertain frequently, but I'm also fairly neat by nature. That isn't to say the odd sock doesn't end up on the coffee table from time to time. Gracie makes herself somewhat comfortable at the kitchen dinette while I scrounge my fridge.

"You don't have to make dinner for me. You weren't expecting me, so it's okay if you want to just talk."

"You need to eat. I'm sure I can rustle something up." I have ground beef thawed and a load of veggies, but I have no clue what to do with that. "Uh, I could make burgers, but I don't have bread. Or maybe spaghetti?"

Gracie peers into the fridge and spies its contents before standing. "You have potatoes?"

I grab the bag from the counter and hold it up.

"Perfect. Cut those up and prep for mashed potatoes while I dice up these carrots and cut that corn off the cob. You have peas?"

"Frozen."

"That works." She goes to work cutting, so I do what I'm told. After she chops up the carrots and mixes them with peas and corn, she dumps the ground beef in a skillet.

"I feel useless. Let me help you." I inch my way into her personal space and steal the spatula from her. She hip-checks me and *kisses* my cheek before letting me take over. I have no idea what she's mixing up beside me, but the heavenly scent of onions and garlic simmering in butter hits me. Whatever she's cooking up will be delicious.

"Here, add this to the ground beef." She offers me the skillet along with a small bowl of mixed herbs. I do as told and continue on. She dumps the veggies in along with some kind of sauce she's made. The whole thing has me drooling, and I don't even know what it is.

"Okay, dump all of that in a casserole and smooth it out. I'm gonna finish the mashed potatoes."

I follow her instructions again and try not to start eating it before it's done. Gracie heaps the mashed potatoes over the top of the mixture, then tops it with cheese. She's speaking the language of a starving man at this point, but apparently, it is not done until it's browned in the oven.

"Alright, we've got twenty minutes until it's done." As soon as she finishes her sentence, it's like she realizes what that means, and all of the light drains from her eyes. She leans against my counter and crosses her arms. I probably shouldn't, but I step in front of her and tip her chin up.

"You don't have to tell me anything you're not ready to share. I'm happy to spend time with you just like this."

Her eyes are swimming again and she bites her lower lip. "My drug-addicted biological parents left me at a police station when I was five. They told me they had to run an errand and would be back. They never came back. Instead, they got clean and had more kids."

Her voice is quiet, clipped, and oh so brutal.

And I get it. Even more than when Nina told me because now I *see* the pain in her eyes, how every word that a person speaks to her might add another layer to that brick wall she's worked so hard to build around her fragile world. When the people who are supposed to love you the most don't, what do you do with that?

"And you think I'll abandon you?" It comes out more strangled than I'd like, but I'm working hard to hold back my own tears. I don't know how anyone can do that to their child. I understand addiction and adoption, and I get that there are many reasons parents might not be able to provide for their child, but to abandon her and then... forget and have a whole other family? I cannot bear how much it must hurt her. How much it *has* hurt her since we were young.

"I don't think you would on purpose, no, but what if—"

"Gracie." I interrupt her. I can't do this. I can't let her keep thinking she's got no one but Nina in her corner. It's not true, and not everyone is like her parents. "It isn't fair that you lump everyone in with your biological parents. We aren't all quitters. We're not all heartless individuals who leave those we care about. Please don't look at me and see someone who is so careless that I will ruin you. You know my family, Gracie. You know how we were raised. What on earth would make you think that I would instigate something with you only to decide later that it's not worth my time?"

Gracie pulls back a little, so I give her space.

"Why now? That's what scares me. Why waste all of those moments between us in the past?"

I groan. "I didn't know, okay? I had no idea I was giving you that feeling, but if I *had* known, I might have behaved differently. I didn't know. I just... I didn't know."

"So at prom, when we were dancing, and you were staring down at me—"

I step forward, halting her question. There's no mistaking that I'm looking at her now. No matter what stupid thing happened at prom, this is what matters. "I thought you looked beautiful. I hated that that stupid guy stood you up because I knew you deserved better than that. I remember thinking I was lucky to have a dance with you. I was staring at you because I did see you, just not the way you wanted back then. I see you that way now, Gracie and I hope that matters."

"It does," she admits. "I don't know what changed, I guess."

I snicker and tap my chin. "Let's see, what might have made me think twice about our relationship? Oh, yes, one minute you were screaming at me, and you called me the world's biggest—"

"I'm sorry! Sorry, don't repeat it," she says, smiling.

"And the next minute, I had you in my arms. Nothing has ever felt that good before, not until a few hours ago in the library. Whether it was a mistake or not doesn't matter. That first kiss got my attention. It woke me up to something I didn't even know I needed, but I want it very much."

"I'm still afraid you'll change your mind."

"I'm not," I whisper. "I want to date you, Gracie Gallagher and I want to show you how right we are together. But what I want doesn't matter. The ball is in your court, and if the answer is no, I'll respect it."

I try to step away, but she's got me by my shirtfront, and a sly grin curves her lips. I've never seen *that* before, and it intrigues me enough to see what happens next. I raise an eyebrow, and I can't help the grin that forms on my own lips. She blushes.

"Used to drive me crazy that you could flash that grin and make all the girls go weak in the knees." She says this and kisses me. Her arms inch up my chest until they're around my neck, pulling me closer.

I'm so happy. I think if I die right now, that will be okay.

Wait. What am I saying?

I definitely do not want to die before I convince this woman that she is worth every ounce of my attention and more. After I achieve that goal, I might just have to prove that I'm not going anywhere and marry her.

Once that m-word hits me, I stiffen. Holy cow. Not those cute little Highland cows Gracie sent to John's house either, but those mean old heifers our grandparents used to raise that chased us through the fields when we were kids. Of course, I meant it when I said I wouldn't abandon Gracie, that I had every intention of sticking around, but it just now hit me what that means. The feeling hasn't changed. I want her. I want a life with her. She's always been here, always a part of my life in some way or another, but the way I want her now is drastically different.

"Paul?" Her voice wavers. She's pulling back, shrinking back into that hole that puts an even bigger space between us.

Whatever nerves I have over this are mine to manage later. Nothing says we have to get married tomorrow.... next year... There is no timeframe. We can grow closer, smooth out this new dynamic between us, then we can plunge into forever.

"Paul," she says and shakes me.

"Huh?" I mumble, finally making eye contact with her. She's terrified. I lean forward and kiss her again, soft and slow, with as much reassurance as I can muster. I'm freaking out a little on the inside, but I didn't lie to her. I'm not going anywhere. She melts against me again, easing back into our kisses after a minor glitch.

Then the buzzer on the oven goes off, and I leap away from her like I just got caught by my parents.

"Geez, that scared me," she said, laughing.

"Me too. Come here." I yank her against me and kiss her one last time, then release her so she can retrieve our dinner.

"Perfect," she says and puts it on the top of the stove. "Cottage pie. Cecily taught me how to make it."

"Oh, Christian's wife?"

"Yep. It's so good."

I can't help myself. Now that she's here and open to me, I can't stop kissing her. I ease in behind her and wrap my arms around her waist, resting my head on her shoulder. I might steal a few neck kisses and nuzzles while she tries to dish up our food. She giggles, and it hits me completely differently than it ever did before.

"Dinner can wait," I proclaim, then spin her around and dive in for another kiss.

She puts on the brakes. "Um, no. My stomach is about to growl, and it will not be attractive in any way, shape, or form. Let's eat, then we can discuss the terms of this dating arrangement."

"Really?" I'm not even a little ashamed at how much hope is in my tone. I feel like I'm a teenage boy again, and I might have just scored the prettiest girl in school.

"Yeah. I think I should stop trying to control everything and let God lead this one."

I accept the plate she's offering me and kiss her cheek. "I think that sounds like a good idea for both of us."

Chapter Eleven
Gracie

I'M NOT UNCOMFORTABLE, BUT this new dynamic with Paul doesn't exactly make me have the cozies, either. I mean, I have warm and snuggly feelings, but I don't trust them. And that's the problem, really, because it isn't his fault I don't trust it. He hasn't given me any reason to doubt what he has said, but when you're used to things being a certain way, it's almost impossible to believe it can be any other way.

"I think you might be overthinking," May says.

I had a minor freakout when I arrived at her home and realized I'd be alone with Paul again. After dinner the night before, we talked and decided to take things slow. We would exclusively date and work toward building deeper trust and understanding. I couldn't ask for more, but it turns out that letting God lead is harder for me than I had anticipated.

May offered to ride along as a buffer, which is really a nice way of saying she'd play the third wheel so I could sort through my feelings a little more. John was working hard getting his new practice up and going, so we didn't bother him to go along. May doesn't have any more appointments, so our late afternoon is full of horseback riding and relaxation. Only I'm not relaxed. All day long, Shelby hounded me about what happened between Paul and me. I never should have told her that I asked him to pick me up, but when he *also* dropped me off at work this morning, she had questions.

"I know I am," I admit.

For some reason, maybe because May is just a sweet person who is easy to talk to, I filled her in on my past—most of it. I didn't tell her about every single moment I *thought* I had with Paul, just the highlights.

"You know he's been asking Calliope and me for advice, right?"

I glance ahead where Paul is, ensuring our path is clear. He's a decent rider, though he never used to be when we were younger. I remember him getting thrown more than once for his poor horsemanship skills.

"I did not."

"Well, he has. I can personally attest to the fact that he has been worried sick about things with you since that first kiss. I also feel pretty confident in saying he's enough like his brothers, that I would trust him with your heart. You've known him longer than I have, though. Is there a reason you believe differently?"

She glances at me and smiles. May is insightful and has a way of calling you on your junk without seeming harsh or intrusive. I've been had, and I know it. Whether the moments between us in the past were a figment of my imagination or not, it does not change the fact that Paul has many good attributes. I let my mind wander back over the years, and I easily pick out so many sweet things he has done for me. So many times, he tried to bury the hatchet between us, even if only for Nina's sake. He's a good brother. A good friend, and I wish I had seen these things sooner. I wish I had recognized what he was doing all along.

"I think he has tried to be my friend, but we were always on different wavelengths. Once when we were—"

"Uh, Gracie?" Paul's tone is not a good sign that he is doing well up ahead. "How do you stop this thing?" he screeches, then he's just gone. Whoops, see you later, out of sight, gone on the back of my horse. Fortunately, it's my sweetest mare, so I'm almost sure she will forgive him for whatever he did wrong and slow down. I think.

May's eyes go wide. "You better—"

"Yeah. Be back in a few," I say and high tail after him. Somehow, he managed to escape the wooded trail and found himself in the open pasture behind John's farm. I'm almost positive it connects to another person's property in only a few hundred yards, but Paul isn't slowing down. "Pull back!" I shout, but I don't think he hears me. I wait until I'm almost alongside him, then shout again. "Pull back, Paul!"

He finally remembers he has control of the situation and does what I say, easing the horse to a stop. My poor baby is frothing like crazy and wild-eyed as can be. What on earth?

Paul pats her on her back and makes wide motions with his hands. "Sna-snake. Fell on us. Was awful," he pants.

"A snake? It fell out of a tree?"

He nods, and I understand. They both freaked out, and this is where it got them.

"Well, you did a nice job stopping once you remembered you could." I grin and reach to scratch my horse's neck. She grumbles a little but doesn't pull away.

Paul snickers and looks out over the field. "Lots of things to jump out here. I remember when we were kids, Nina would drag me along with her to watch your competitions. I admit, it was boring to me then, but I realize now how hard it must be."

"You came to my meets?" How had I missed that?

"Um, yeah. You don't remember always getting hot dogs after? Every time your meet ended, we went to Hot Dog Haven, and I always got sick."

I smile. I do remember, and it's one more moment that warms my heart. "I remember. You ate six one time and—"

"Ugh, don't remind me. I puked out the window. It was awful."

"Oh, I remember. You splattered like three cars behind us. Your mother was so embarrassed." I can't hold back my laughter now.

"I'm glad my pain is funny to you." Paul closes the distance between us and kisses my cheek. "Are you okay? I got the feeling you were a little stressed when our ride began, so if you need some alone time, I get it."

Why am I making this so hard on myself? He's so sweet, and he's done nothing to warrant mistrust in any way. Yet, I cannot seem to cut that last thread of doubt that this is all temporary, and soon enough, he will find a reason to walk away. To abandon me. My jaw clenches. No. I will not do this. I will not project my uncertainty onto him.

"I'm fine. I actually think I want to do some of these jumps. Want to ride around with me and make sure it's safe enough?"

"I think I'll sit right here for a few minutes if you don't mind." Paul wipes his brow, but I don't miss the queasiness in his expression before he tries to hide it. "Here comes May."

She emerges from the trees in a lazy trot. I notice her form is amazing. Paul, on the other hand, must have forgotten every single lesson I ever gave him. This does not surprise me in the least. I head towards a felled tree and inspect it, then ride around a few more potential jumps. Once everything looks good, I decide to go for it. It's been a long while since Elsa, my mare, and I have had a good run. She seems excited and willing, so we make a run around the field and line up for the first jump. We sail over it with ease and cut towards the next, but a flock of birds darts from a patch of tall grass and spooks her. We're going pretty fast when she decides to cut and run, and rather than try to hold on for dear life and hurt us both, I exit stage left and fall from her back.

It's not the first time I've taken a nosedive, but I forgot that the others don't know it's common, and a good rider knows how to fall without breaking her neck. Paul slides onto his knees beside me just as I'm sitting up. He's in full panic mode, eyes wide, and hands checking me over like one might a small child who took a spill.

"Gracie! Gracie, are you alright?" He's cupped my face now, eyes wild with worry.

"Hey, it's okay. I'm completely fine. I bailed on purpose."

His eyes narrow but he doesn't let me go. "You fell on purpose?"

"Well, yeah. It's better to bail and control my fall than have my scared horse throw me. I know how to fall. I promise I'm alright."

"Are you sure?" His thumbs brush over my cheekbones. He's genuinely worried, but that was never a problem with him. Paul is always worried about his friends, and he's always been the first one to step up and take care of us.

"I really am," I whisper. "But it's kinda cute how worried you are." I lean forward and give him a quick kiss before wiggling free to find Elsa. She's nibbling grass in the same place where the birds burst out and scared us. Silly mare. "We should head back so they can get a drink and eat. Next time, maybe I'll get all the way around the course before trying a superhero stunt."

"You better not do a superhero stunt in front of me again. That was terrifying, Gracie."

I slip my hand into his while we walk toward the horses. May is already crossing the field, heading back toward the pasture. The woman is so tuned into other people, it's a little freaky, but she clearly saw a moment coming and left us to have it alone. Then again, since it seems I have been such a poor judge of the moments between Paul and me, I try not to put too much thought into it.

Paul tugs my hand and pulls me against his chest. "Terrifying, but you're still the best rider. Even the flying was graceful."

"They don't call me Gracie for nothing, you know."

"That's not even funny," he teases.

"It was all I had." I grab Elsa's reins and mount while Paul gets settled on Anna. I was on an animated movie kick when I bought them both, but the names perfectly fit their personalities. Elsa is frigid with everyone but me, while Anna never met a stranger she didn't immediately fall in love with. Paul is no exception. She nibbles his rear when he tries to get on, and the most girlish yelp echoes in the field. I can't help giggling while his face turns bright red. Anna goes in for another nibble, and he leaps away.

"Okay, not funny. Stay away from the private parts, Anna!"

My mare shakes her mane out, which is funny in itself, but Paul takes advantage of her distraction and settles in the saddle before she can take another bite out of him. He glances up at me with a scowl he doesn't mean. I can tell the difference, having been on the receiving end of quite a few of his scathing glares.

"Why do I feel like you put me on this horse on purpose?"

"Nah. If I wanted to torture you, I would have put you on Spice. She's got the red-headed personality down pat."

"Like you? I like my women a little spicy," he says, winking.

I roll my eyes and join him in a meandering walk back to the pasture. "Okay, I walked into that one, I admit, but you once told me that you hate redheads."

He huffs out a snort. "I lied."

"So, when we played that group game of twenty questions, and Rhodes asked you who your ideal girl was, you lied?"

Paul laughs and covers his mouth. His eyes crinkle, and there's nothing but pure joy in this memory. It was a fun game and one of the rare moments we got along for more than ten minutes. We were about seventeen, in junior year of high school, and both of our friend groups were at the Loughton house hanging out.

"What?" I insist, smiling so wide my cheeks hurt.

He can't stop laughing but finally calms enough to admit the truth. "I couldn't exactly sit there and describe my ideal woman when one was literally sitting in the circle with us. Rhodes and the other guys would have given me such a hard time, okay?"

"Oh, please. We both know a short little thing with red hair and blue eyes was *not* your type in high school, Paul." I don't mind his teasing now because the spirit in which it is intended isn't cruel. Not that it ever was, really. I realize now that cruelty was *never* intended. That our misunderstandings were silly, youthful mistakes that I never should have taken so seriously... especially as we got older and they were fewer and farther between.

I'm so lost in thought that I don't notice he's not cracking up anymore.

"Gracie, just because I dated a few girls who looked different from you doesn't mean I didn't think you were beautiful. That was never one of the issues between us." He reaches for me and squeezes my knee. "I still think you're beautiful. You're kind of a rarity, you know."

True. I *was* the only redhead in our school at the time, so he's probably right. Describing someone who looks like me was bound to raise an eyebrow. People would have been trying to set us up left and right. On second thought, I kind of wish he had admitted his type back then.

"Hey, you're quiet," he says. "Did I say something wrong?"

"What?" I jerk my head towards him. "No, of course not. I was just thinking. Thank you for telling me that."

"For telling you that I was so freaked out during a game of twenty questions that I lied about how beautiful I thought you were? You're welcome." He's chuckling again, and I pray it can always be this way between us. I like the laughter way more than the arguments.

I maneuver my horse so we move ahead just a little, then turn her so I can face Paul. This stops both horses, and we're looking at each other. I inhale and remind myself that this is okay. He's been open and accepting and so patient with me, and I'm beginning to see all of the little mistakes along the way don't matter... even my dead hamster. Even now, waiting for me to speak, I have his attention and his patience.

"I should have said this a long time ago. If I had, then maybe we wouldn't have spent so many years taunting and annoying each other. I, Gracie Gallagher, have the biggest crush on you, Paul Loughton, and I'm sorry that I've been kind of a booger about it."

Paul's smile reaches his eyes again, and he leans forward to kiss me... or so I thought. Instead, he raises his lips to my ear and says... "I know." Then bolts. The jerk takes off and screams, "Race you!" as he's barreling toward the pasture.

"Oh, you... you... ugh!" I scream and urge Elsa to kick his rear end.

Unfortunately, between my initial shock and his head start, he's out of sight by the time Elsa and I reach the pasture. I release her from her restraints and turn her loose to drink and graze before heading into the stable to clean up. I have no idea where Paul disappeared to, but once I get my hands on him, I'm gonna give him a piece of my mind. A smile curves on my lips. All this time, his playfulness annoyed me, but now, it makes me a little giddy. He's playing with *me.* Seeking *my* attention.

When I pass a stall, a hand reaches out, and suddenly, I'm tumbling into a pile of straw. I shriek, but Paul's lips are on mine before even a syllable is uttered. I had not considered hiding away in a stall and kissing to be an option, but I find I am not at all opposed to this stolen moment with him. Not even a little.

When he releases me for a breath, that stupid grin gives me chills.

"I won," he whispers. "And in case you wondered, I have a crush on you too."

"Do you?"

Paul kisses my nose. "Of course. Redheads are my thing, after all."

A grumble distracts us from our kissing, and my cheeks instantly heat when I hear John. "There are animals running amuck all over my property. Would you kindly stop making out in my barn and help me catch them!"

Paul and I rush from the stable to find that I had forgotten to close the gate behind me. Goats, ponies, horses, sheep, and one obstinate donkey are literally spread all across his property, causing trouble. May is working hard to convince the hog to get back into his little corral, but he's more interested in eating her tulips. Paul squeezes my waist and offers me a guilty grin before we spend the next two hours herding all of the animals that I sent to John.

Once the final sheep is back in with the flock, John issues me one of *his* signature glares. "If you send another animal here, I will spend the rest of my life making sure you regret it." I know he doesn't mean it, but a chill still shivers down my spine.

"Now, where were we?" Paul asks, urging me towards the barn.

"Just about to head home to shower," I say, earning the worst frown I have ever seen. Paul concedes, but I know there will probably be many more stable kisses in my future. The thought alone makes my cheeks heat as I settle into the passenger seat of his Jeep.

Chapter Twelve

Paul

It occurs to me after spending an afternoon with May, that Gracie might be missing out on something special. Her parents adopted her but didn't adopt any other children, nor did they have any biological children. She's an only child, which isn't a problem in itself, but I wonder if knowing she has siblings out there in the world bothers her. Does she want a connection with them, and would that potentially help her overcome the hurdles she faces every day?

"Is everything okay? Are you upset with me because I said no more kissing?" she asks, glancing at me with pink cheeks.

"Gracie, no. I will never be upset with you over anything like that. I think of myself as a pretty lucky guy that I get to kiss you at all." I glance at her and note that her cheeks are even pinker as she stares out the windshield.

"What is it then? Something is clearly bothering you."

"Promise you won't get mad at me if I tell you? I hate that we've had so many misunderstandings, and I don't want this to turn into one. It comes from a place of genuine concern and care, okay?"

She offers me a warning glance but nods anyway.

"I can't imagine how it must feel to know that your parents got clean and had more children. I don't pretend to understand what that can do to a person, but I wonder if contacting your siblings might..." I wave my hand around, unsure how to say what I'm thinking in a gentle and respectful way that won't upset her more.

She sighs and turns to face me, crossing her arms. She's defensive, but at least it seems like she's willing to talk. "I've thought about what you're insinuating. I'm not even sure if they know I exist, honestly, and I don't want to cause anyone undue trauma."

"That makes sense. Do you think it might help you process things if you had a relationship with them, though? I mean, you can't change what your parents did. If they didn't tell your siblings that you exist, then it's not really your fault if your very existence causes them problems." I know once I say it, it came out all wrong. I'm convinced of that when I catch her arched brow, but rather than scold me and tell me it's none of my business—things she would have done only days ago—she offers me a soft smile.

"I know what you're trying to say... I think... but it isn't that easy. As badly as I'm hurt by their actions, I wouldn't feel comfortable causing that same pain to another person, whether it's my fault it exists or not. Does that make sense?"

I'm so relieved that this didn't blow up into a fight that the weight of it eases off my shoulders. We're really doing this, working through things together, and shockingly, it's working. She's more open to me than she has ever been, and I'm beginning to understand this woman and her needs on another level.

"You know, sometimes I get jealous of how close Edwin and John are, but I still have them in my life, and they have my back all the time. Same with Nina and even Rhodes. It's just a thought, but if you decide you want to reach out to them, you know Nina and I will be right by your side the whole time." She is clearly out of her comfort zone right now, but I also have a feeling that with my sister as her best friend—the woman who spends her days helping abuse victims find their footing again—Gracie might be getting the soft glove treatment a little too much. I adore my sister and what she does for people, but it often extends past her work and into her personal relationships. I get it. It's hard to separate your work life and home life, but part of me wonders if we pushed Gracie a little harder, she might blossom, spread her wings, and soar.

"I see the wheels still turning in that brain of yours. You either want to say more, or you have an opinion on the matter you think will offend me."

I offer a cautious glance her way. She reaches for my hand, so I intertwine my fingers with hers, though driving with one hand gives me indigestion. I get that from Edwin, the guy who taught me how to drive. That was an awful mistake, but it happened, and now I suffer the consequences of hearing his voice scolding me whenever I break a rule.

"I want to always be honest with each other now. If this is going to work, then I think you should say what you want to say, and I will try my hardest to accept it in the spirit in which it is intended." And then she braces for impact. I feel her tense, so I squeeze her hand.

"The spirit intended is with love, Gracie. Whether we're together or not, you're family and I care about you."

"But?" she asks.

"But I think maybe you stay in such a small comfort zone, it sort of... I don't know. It keeps you in a place that doesn't allow for much growth. Does that make sense?" I don't miss the flare in her eyes as she absorbs what I say, but I also note how quickly her expression softens again. "I want you to be happy, and whether that is through reaching out to your siblings or not is up to you. Just don't hold yourself back from exploring the possibilities because the consequences are too scary."

"I'm exploring this with you, aren't I? That's way out of my comfort zone, and the consequences are the most terrifying I've ever faced, honestly."

Okay, she's not wrong. I hadn't really thought of how far out of comfort she had to travel to meet me, even halfway. "Fair enough. That's true, but I have to say that I love seeing you smile, and it makes me want to find all the things that will make you happy and do them with you."

She bites her lower lip, and her eyes flutter to look down at her lap. I bite my tongue and decide to let her work through everything on her own. If she needs me, she'll ask for my help. Otherwise, I'll just let it simmer and see what happens. The rest of the way to her place, we exist in quiet contemplation until I pull into her drive. She left her car, complete with a fresh new battery, at John's on purpose so she could drive her truck and trailer over for them to use as needed on the farm, then she could drive her car back. We have been rearranging things left and right, trying to get Gracie's property back in order, but I know it feels off for her. Her whole routine is out of whack, so really, she's farther from her comfort zone than I had considered. An apology is on the tip of my tongue as I park.

"Listen, I probably had no right telling you to step out of your place of—"

Gracie moves across my seat and kisses me. There are worse ways to be interrupted, so I give in and kiss her. She's comfortable now, judging by the sweet softness of this kiss, and I hope things between us stay this way... grow deeper... build something solid. Then she releases me with a sweet smile.

"You do have a right to tell me those things for my own good. I'm not upset, and I actually think I might want to put some feelers out and see what's involved with contacting them."

"Do you know where they live?"

"They live in upstate South Carolina, not too far. I thought I could ask Nina to reach out to some people there, see if any of them have done the same. I mean, we're talking about kids here. The oldest is just now eighteen. There's a chance I won't be able to do anything for a few years."

"That's true," I admit. I hadn't thought about that, and her rationale for wanting to be careful about the disruption in their lives hits me a lot differently now. It would be awful to bulldoze into the lives of a few teenagers, especially if they have no idea Gracie exists. "Whatever you want to do, I'll support you."

"I know, and I appreciate that more than you can know." She kisses my cheek and unbuckles. "I'd invite you in, but all I'm going to do is shower, eat dinner, and crash. Is that okay?"

"Yep. Another date soon?"

"Of course. I'll let you know my schedule, and we'll plan. Also, I have to get back in touch with Edwin about the barn. I think I'm ready for that phase, especially since a lot of the old wood was salvageable. That, combined with what I had already bought for repairs, might be close to enough."

My phone rings, so I dig it out of my pocket. "It's John. I should take it, but I'll talk to you soon." I lean over and steal another kiss before she slides from my truck and heads inside.

"What's up, big bro?" I ask by way of answering his call.

"Small problem and I need your help. I'm gonna need another assistant for something May wants to do."

"I thought you had an assistant. Bev, isn't it?"

"Yes, and she's great, but this is a big project, and I'll need someone on it full-time."

"I'm not sure what that has to do with me. I'm a history teacher. I cannot help you run a law firm while I grade papers."

John sighs. "Not you. Putting you in charge of anything here would get me disbarred in a blink. I have an idea. I've been thinking about this since Gracie sent the sheep. Actually, it was May's idea, but the logistics of it have been a nightmare. She thought about starting a therapy farm, and Nina has been giving us pointers on how to go about working with local therapists, but May just doesn't have the time to do it on her own."

"I'm still not sure what that has to do with me."

"I'm running on empty here trying to get my firm well rooted. Bev is already working sixty hours a week helping, and May really wants to do this. She's invested, but time is a problem."

"I thought May really wanted to be a beautician, hence the salon on your property." I'm so confused I realize I'm still sitting in Gracie's driveway. Still, John not making sense usually means he has something in mind that will blow you away, so sitting still rather than driving is probably a good idea.

"She enjoys it, yes, but sometimes you find a calling that fits you better than you ever thought possible. I know the feeling pretty well. She's still setting up her shop for now, but if we can get the therapy farm started, it would be a dream come true for her."

I chuckle. There is literally not a thing my big brother will not do for May Hollis, and it is both sweet and terrifying at the same time. The woman has power most of us can only covet, and all she has to do is smile at her fiancé. "Okay, so what do you need me to do?"

"I think you know what I want you to do, but you're playing dumb, so you don't have to do it." I literally have no idea. The silence lasts long enough to annoy John, so he grumbles his usual bearish growl and says, "Ask Gracie if she would be interested in a full-time position helping May on the farm, doofus."

"Oh! Gracie, yeah, that makes... Wait, why don't you ask her yourself? It's not like you never see her, and she—"

"Are you sure you're Edwin's and my brother? You do not have a romantic bone in your body, you doofus. I'm giving you the opportunity to offer the woman you love a dream job, one that I already know she will love based on May's probing questions this afternoon."

"But she likes working at the library," I say, then my mind drifts towards the booger books and flooded, duck-infested lobby. "Okay, but you're the one offering her employment, not me."

"Well, May and I are willing to slightly alter the facts to fit a story that says it was more your idea than ours."

"You mean lie to Gracie. Nope, I'm not doing that, but thanks. I'll mention it to her."

"Suit yourself. Whatever she's making at the library, tell her I'll add twenty-five percent to start. Once the farm earns some clients and can stand on its own, I'll give her a raise. She can call me for more details about benefits and all of that if she's interested."

"Yeah, okay," I say, stunned. My brother has always been generous, but since May walked into his life, he's been giving away his things left and right. He offers a few grunts and pleasantries before hanging up.

I can't decide if I should barge in and mention it to Gracie now or wait until I see her again. I give her some time alone to work through all of the things we talked about rather than throw one more offer on her plate. As I drive home, I work through the logistics of telling her, trying to figure out how to do it in a way that doesn't seem like complete charity from the Loughton family to her.

It's probably true that it's a lot of work, and May will need help, and there's no denying that Gracie knows how to care for animals. Frankly, it's probably the most amazing job for her, but that doesn't mean she'll want the charity. It was difficult enough to get her to let me help her tear down the barn.

When I finally make it home, I'm exhausted, so I eat and get ready for bed, all the while plotting and planning how to present this job offer to Gracie without overwhelming her.

Then it hits me.

I'm giving you the opportunity to offer the woman you love a dream job.

The word love fell right out of my brother's mouth with all the casualness of a simple statement, but it held so much more weight than that. I hadn't noticed it, hadn't caught what he said, and never denied it. I don't want to deny it, though I'm not completely sure that's how I feel just yet. But it is the goal. I want to be open enough to Gracie that love naturally follows, and everything else falls in line after that. It was such a simple prayer in church, but every part of it seems to be falling into place.

Chapter Thirteen
Gracie

AFTER EATING LIKE A starving monkey and showering, I sit down to call Edwin about the barn. Via email, he said he might be able to help me design something efficient and inexpensive, so all of my hope hinges on his magnificent design abilities. Edwin has always been kind to me, even if he is a bit stuffy, but ever since Calliope entered the picture, he's been less and less grumpy—still particular as ever, but less cranky about it.

"Hello, Gracie. How are you?"

"Tired, you?"

"Exhausted with wedding planning, so coming up with ideas for your barn was a nice break. I talked with an architect friend of mine, and we have some ideas. You said eight stalls would be sufficient, and I have a few sketches that might work. We went with more of a square structure to limit the need for structural beams and—"

"Okay, you lost me after sketches," I admit.

He chuckles. "Well, I'll just say it might not strike you as a typical barn design, but given your needs and budget, I have three designs that might work. My friend owes me a favor, so he's going to draft the final plans based on the one you choose. I'll email the sketches and rough plans tonight, and you can let me know which you like best tomorrow."

"Are you serious? Edwin, you don't need to go wasting favors on me!"

"Nonsense. You're family, Gracie."

The way it slips from his mouth without question warms my heart. Edwin is honest and forthright, even a little blunt when it comes to the truth. I wonder if I should ask him about all of the things that terrify me.

"Ed... Edwin, can I... Would it be weird for me to ask you a question about your relationship with Calliope?"

"I think it depends on the question, but go for it."

I settle into my sofa and consider how to word my thoughts so he doesn't think I'm nuts. I'm also not crazy about digging deep into my abandonment issues with him, especially since he doesn't know about my biological parents moving on with a big new family.

"I guess I want to know what made you realize she was the right person for you. How were you able to let go and let her in?"

The line is quiet for a while, and I think maybe he's annoyed with me. Whatever he is doing on the other end of the line requires tapping a pen on a desk or something similar because the incessant noise echoes through the phone.

"She understands me. It's like she's three steps ahead, and she's willing to adjust to help me just be me. Because of that, I want to do the same for her. We simply make adjustments for one another out of love, and it clicks."

"I see," I say, thinking over everything Paul has done for me lately. He's tried, and he's done everything possible to make life easier for me during this crazy time. Have I done the same for him? Have I thought of his needs and tried to adjust to make him happy, too? Maybe a little by merely trying to trust him, but I'm not sure I'm ready to dive any deeper than that. I'm too scared.

"Are you alright, Gracie?" Edwin's tone has slipped into the one that says he's going to give me advice if I don't pretend everything is peachy keen. Still, maybe some brotherly advice would be nice, even if it's about to be brutally honest.

"I'm struggling, if I'm honest."

"Is Paul pushing you too much?"

"No, not at all. He's been great, which is what scares me. It's a long story, but trust is hard for me."

"Your fear of abandonment?"

My mouth falls open. "How... how did you know?"

Edwin chuckles again. "One thing about the prickly types is that we tend to pay close attention to everything because it might cause us discomfort if we are surprised. I've noticed over the years that when things require commitment, you tend to flee. It's not a judgment, mind you, just an observation that is understandable.

Honestly, it's quite normal for those adopted to struggle with placement and abandonment issues."

"So, I'm not crazy if I'm terrified of losing him and all of you in the process?"

"Well, no matter what happens between you and my brother, you can't lose us all. You are stuck with the Loughton family, like it or not, but no, you are not crazy. Incidentally, Paul is the only one who was clueless when it came to you. The rest of us knew how you felt about him. I apologize that my brother is not an observant man, but despite that pitfall, he is loyal, Gracie. He is loyal to a fault, trustworthy, and though he may not be the best planner, when he commits, it is for the long haul."

I try to relax and trust Edwin. Of anyone, he likely knows how I feel. His idiot ex left him three days before their wedding, but I'm glad for it now. Calliope is the best, and I can't imagine anyone better than her for Edwin. The same goes for May and John. Now, if I could only convince myself that I am as deserving as Calliope and May, maybe I will get somewhere.

"Have you talked with him about this?" Edwin asks.

"Yes, he knows about my concerns."

"And has he addressed them?"

"Yes, at length, actually. He claims he's not going anywhere, but how can he be sure? We've only been dating a day, Edwin."

"Dating a day, but in each other's orbit for many, many years. Paul is not one to toy with a woman's emotions. Perhaps his nerves make him a bit free with his flirting, but if he has said he is not leaving you, then he isn't. Unless, of course, you force him to by telling him to get lost. I beg you not to do that. He will likely be insufferable judging by his moping the past few months."

I can't help but laugh at Edwin's delivery. It's the truth, but he has a way of saying things that make me laugh even when he's not trying to.

"My brother is solid. This has been a long time coming. Enjoy it if you can, Gracie, because falling in love with the one God made for you is worth every precious moment of your attention."

Falling in love? My heart races, especially when my brain reminds me that what he said is true. It snuck up on me over the years, perhaps, but now it's peeking out to test the waters. Love. Holy cow, I'm falling in love with him.

"Thank you, Edwin."

"Anytime. I'll email those plans, and let me know what you like. We can make any adjustments you need."

"Perfect. I really appreciate the plans and the advice more than you know," I admit.

"You're going to be alright, Gracie. Paul is a good place to land. Goodnight," he whispers just before hanging up.

Paul is a good place to land.

I let his words roll over in my mind until I see it. I believe it, and it gives me enough confidence to make a phone call I never thought I would make. Nina answers after a few rings. She's exhausted, judging by her strained voice, but she tries to seem cheerful for me.

"Hey, Gracie! What's up?"

"I want to do something that might be crazy, and I need your help."

"Okay, should I be scared?"

"Well... I want to reach out to my biological family and see if I can meet my siblings. I know it seems like a stupid thing to do considering all of my issues, but it isn't their fault, right?"

"You want to reach out to them? Now?"

Her tone has taken a sharp turn, and it deflates my whole heart. "Shouldn't I?"

"I just think... I mean, there's a lot involved, especially since they are minors. Only one is of age to make a decision on his own. Do you really want to intrude into their lives at such a young age?" Nina's work makes me think she's probably right. She deals with trauma for a living, so she would know when a person's actions might have a negative impact on others. After all, it was my fear as well.

"I guess not. Paul suggested—"

Nina's sigh interrupts me. "Paul always means well, but sometimes he doesn't think about the ramifications of his actions. I'm absolutely sure his suggestion comes from a good place in his heart, but he doesn't understand how these things can impact people for the long term, especially children."

"Oh... Well, I guess..."

"I suggest waiting a while. I can email a friend in social services and let her put out some feelers. That way, if any of them try to contact you, they will know you are willing to see them. Does that sound okay?"

"Yeah... I... I guess so," I say, my heart already aching at losing something I never even had.

"Okay, I'll get on that first thing in the morning. Listen, I love Paul, but when it comes to things like this, he just doesn't know what he doesn't know, okay? I think it's great that you two are working things out and seeing how your relationship can grow, but don't dive in too deep too fast."

My stomach rumbles with nerves. She's probably right. I shouldn't let this new relationship with Paul dictate how my life works. I've always been cautious for a reason—a good reason—so leaping off of a cliff now seems like a horrible idea.

"I think he had good intentions," I say.

"I do, too. Just trust me, though, okay?"

"Yeah, I guess you're right. Sorry, I bothered you so late."

"I was up. It's not a problem. Want to go shopping with me this weekend? I need to pick up my bridesmaid dress from the alteration shop and find some shoes. Have you gotten a dress yet?"

Oh yes, the wedding. Going alone to the wedding seemed like an okay idea only a few weeks ago, but now that I'm in a haphazard relationship with Paul, I'm not so sure. He hasn't asked me, which brings up a whole new load of confusion and nervous energy. But I can't let Nina know I'm worried about that, or she'll dive into a speech I'm not feeling right now.

"Yeah, that will be fine. See you Saturday?"

"Yep, love you!"

"Me too," I whisper and hang up. Suddenly, I know what birthday balloons feel like. Popped, useless, and shriveled.

I climb into bed a little worse for the wear and try to think of what I'll tell Paul. I know he will have an opinion on the matter, but I don't want to spark a fight between siblings. With a restless mind and heart, I drift to sleep with so many more things to worry about than ever before.

Chapter Fourteen
Paul

"ARE YOU INSANE?" I stare back at the dozens of eyeballs looking at me as if, somehow, their signed petition might actually get them out of the test. Thirty-three signatures, and not one student—including the one who thinks she's smarter than me—was prepared for the test I had been warning them would be difficult for the past month. "I'm serious right now. Are you all insane?"

"We didn't have enough time to prepare," one says, but judging by his tone, he knows it's a last-ditch effort.

"Tough. I told you a *month* ago that you would have a test on this topic and that it was difficult. It is not my fault that you chose to put other things at the top of your priority list. Pencils out, lips zipped, and do your best."

"But—"

"If you stop whining now, I *might* grade on a curve."

All eyes go to the smarty pants kid, who would absolutely destroy that curve for everyone. Let her take the heat for them not taking history seriously. It's totally not my fault they didn't pay attention, and at this point, I'd be perfectly happy to make them learn it all over again."

I pass the tests out amid grumbles and whines, but I ignore them. It's not the first time, and it won't be the last.

"Mr. Loughton, can we use our textbooks?" someone asks.

My head almost spins. Why do these kids constantly seek a free pass? No one ever wants to put the work in and study anymore, and I've had all I can take of wasting my time day after day, standing at the front of the class lecturing to no one like an idiot. I groan and toss the extra tests onto my desk.

"I'll tell you what. You have a choice. Take the test without your textbook, or use your textbook, but write a five-page essay about the impact the initial phase of the war had on America."

"Five pages?" The whining has begun in earnest now, and many see the benefit of simply attempting the test and digging deep into the recesses of their brain for the answers.

"Time's ticking. Tick tock," I say.

The hour passes with a lot of furious erasing, but overall, I'm pleased with my hardline stance—you're at school, do the work. Seven decided to write essays, which I'm actually pretty impressed by, while the rest drop their mostly completed tests in a haphazard pile on my desk after the bell rings. I'll be up half the night grading those essays, but it might restore my hope in the future if any of them are actually good.

I check my phone and see that Nina had messaged me, so during my planning period, I return her call. I don't expect annoyance when she answers.

"What were you thinking?" she asks instead of saying hello.

"I have no idea what I did to set you off today, but I'll hang up on you if you don't chill. I've got six classes of students peeved about a test and literally no patience left for snarky comments from my sister."

"It's not my fault you teach a boring subject, but I warned you to be careful with Gracie. Why would you encourage her to reach out to her biological family after everything they did to her?"

I huff and try not to tell my sister to take a leap. "I suggested she reach out to her siblings. I can't say why now, but at the time, I was thinking about how wonderful it is to have them."

"You're not funny. They are minors, and that means we would have to reach out to her parents to see them. Did you even think about how that could hurt her? I had to burst her bubble last night after your bright idea."

To hear Nina speak, you'd think Gracie was a moron who couldn't think for herself, and I'm beginning to see why she might be so reserved and afraid. With a best friend like my sister, it's entirely possible she hasn't thought for herself about her issues in a long time, if ever.

"Nina, I love you, and I say this with absolute respect for you and what you do for a living, but back off. Gracie was fine with my suggestion, and it wasn't like I had a gun to her head. She said she wasn't sure, so I told her whatever she decided was fine, and I'd support her either way."

"Do not tell me to back off when my best—"

"Stop treating her like a child or a client! She isn't your charity case, Nina. She's a grown woman who seriously lacks confidence, partially because people keep treating her like she might break."

"Well, you don't know how hard it was for her!" She's yelling now, which hits me all wrong. I don't *want* to fight with my sister, but over this, I absolutely will. Rhodes' voice echoes in the background, but I can't make out what he says. Our friend since high school has known the good and bad sides of all of us and often gets stuck in the middle of these disagreements.

"You're right. I don't, but I'm trying to understand and maybe give her a different perspective," I say.

"You just started dating her, and suddenly you think you know what she needs better than I do? You don't. You only know what little she's told you, not the whole story."

I know I won't get anywhere when she's like this, stuck in overprotective friend mode, so I take a few breaths and try to calm down. She says nothing, but I hear her doing the same on the other end. Finally, I venture into conversation again.

"It isn't as if I don't care about her, and I do respect your work, but that doesn't mean that what I said isn't valid. When we're together, Gracie opens up a lot. She laughs and has fun, and I'm trying to be here for her, but honestly, if she isn't moving forward, then where does that leave her?"

Nina is still silent, but Rhodes' hushed voice seems to be soothing her. All I can make out are bits of his argument that perhaps neither of us is right or wrong, but the situation is just complicated. He's probably right, but I'm still annoyed.

"Look, I'll apologize to her, and I won't bring it up again, but I think you should look at what your position in this might be. I have no doubt you mean well, but is it really your place to dictate her life so much?"

Click.

That's it. Nothing more. She hung up without a word.

I have very little reason to believe what I'm about to do won't blow up in my face, but I do it anyway. I call Gracie at the library. The only way to know whether or not my suggestion caused her any harm is to ask her myself and completely cut my sister out as the middleman.

"Hi, it's nice to get a call from you in the middle of the day," Gracie says—a much better hello than my sister's.

"If that's the kind of greeting I'll get, I'll call you every day. It's my planning period, so I can totally swing it. Better than grading tests any day."

Gracie chuckles. "What's up?"

"I just talked to Nina. Listen, I'm sorry if suggesting you reach out to your siblings caused you any discomfort. I was just trying to help you move forward, but if it's not my lane, then you can tell me, and I'll swerve back into mine."

"She raked you over the coals, didn't she?"

"A little, but it's fine. She loves you and doesn't want you to get hurt."

Gracie sighs, and a door shuts in the background. "I know, but can I tell you a secret? I went behind her back and reached out anyway. I talked to a social services representative today, and she said it's possible to reach out to them with feelers and see if they are interested in setting something up either now or maybe later if they haven't told the kids about me. I'm nervous, but I woke up this morning feeling like it was the right thing to do."

My heart swells, and I'm so proud of her. I had been worried that Nina's intrusion might set her back, but it seems I was wrong. Gracie has a much better grasp on her independence than I had realized. A wash of shame spreads over my cheeks, warming them. I should have had more confidence in her, but I won't make that mistake again.

"I'm so happy for you, and no matter what happens, I'm here."

"I know. That's why I did it anyway. I'll probably be sick over it for a while, but it'll be worth it if they want to meet. If not, then I guess I'll know, and I can stop thinking about them and why they did what they did."

"How very mature of you," I tease, trying to keep things light so she doesn't get too stressed thinking about either option.

"Ha, ha. Listen, Shelby is wrangling kids all over, so I gotta go help her, but maybe come by after work?"

"Hmm, do I get to knock over some more bookcases with you?"

"No, but I could maybe arrange for dinner and meaningful conversation," she teases.

"Fine, fine. I'll take what I can get. See you later."

She yells to her coworker that she's coming before hanging up, and I release a breath. Thank goodness she's not angry with me, but I can't help worrying that somehow Nina will get wind that Gracie went behind her back, and I'm gonna catch all kinds of words for it. No one ever told me about the complications of dating your sister's best friend, but even if they had, I probably wouldn't have listened.

I make my way through the pile of tests, some of which are decent, then land on an essay written by my arch-nemesis—my new one since Gracie and I moved beyond glares and into kissing—and it's a doozy. Evidently, a five-page essay outlining why I am the worst history teacher in the history of teaching took priority over actually doing the assignment. I take great joy in writing the big, fat, red "F" on her paper. The principal will be involved in this, I'm sure, since this particular student pulls this sort of thing with all of the teachers. There is no denying her intelligence, but that ego needs a big check, and I'm just annoyed enough to make sure she gets it.

Chapter Fifteen
Gracie

CHAPTER FIFTEEN

Gracie

"Get off the phone with your hot boyfriend and help me," Shelby scolds from the kindergarten room. This time, we have contained the crazy to one room rather than allowing it to run rampant all over the library. We also ensured the teacher would play an active part in the disciplinary process. However, even with basic safeguards, we have found ourselves entirely overwhelmed by little people and their sticky fingers. Unfortunately, they are adorable little people who happen to be difficult to hold accountable for their spectacular wall art.

"Hey, don't talk about my boyfriend that way," I say and blush. He really is handsome, and a little giddiness tickles my stomach. He's sweet and thoughtful, and I wish I had seen those things all along. I see them now, looking back, but perhaps if I had given him a chance all these years, we might have ended up together a lot sooner.

Or maybe it all happened the way it was supposed to.

"You okay?" Shelby asks. It's barely a whisper over the children, but she moves closer to chat. She's not exactly schooled in all things Gracie's life, but she knows I was adopted.

"I reached out to see if my biological siblings might want to meet, so I'm a little on edge, I think. Trying not to have expectations either way."

Her gray eyes widen and she wants to say something, but instead, she gets splatted upside the head with slime.

"I'm so sorry. They think they can do anything after last week's class told them all about the library," the teacher said, but at least she's more invested in her children's behavior than the last teacher. "I don't even know how they got slime."

"Come on, I'll help you get it out of your hair before you make a huge mess," I say, grabbing Shelby by the arm before she socks a small, laughing child.

"No more. No more children's field trips, and I mean it. I will quit and run so far, so fast, you'll see dust behind me." I don't blame her, truly, because the last two field trips have been a nightmare. Three, actually. There was a group of high school students who spent the entire hour talking as loudly as possible, which thoroughly upset the elderly ladies' romance book club. They also left their snack wrappers all over and didn't put a single book back where it came from.

In the bathroom, she gets to work cleaning slime from her hair, but she also gives me an expectant stare. "Well, go on."

"I mean, that's it. Paul suggested I see if they might want to meet. Nina thought it was a terrible idea, but I did it anyway. Something told me I needed to give it a try, so now I just wait." I shrug, but my little heart is pounding. Rejection could come any day, but so might acceptance. I can't even decide which would be better at this point.

"It's definitely surprising, but I think I agree with Paul." Shelby's pulling her hair out strand by strand, so I hold the already cleaned parts away from the mess.

"You don't even know what he said."

"No, but if it involves you making connections with family, I think it's good for you. I adore you, and I'd love to see you have more people in your life who are aware of how amazing you are. You're a good friend, sweet, and you're fun to be around. There's no reason your siblings should want to avoid you."

"Well, all but one is a minor, so it's really not up to me. It's up to my biological parents, and they haven't really been in the picture." I've given her a good bit of insight into my world now, but it doesn't seem to faze her.

"Everyone's got a story, Gracie. There isn't a human alive who hasn't been let down, disappointed, or downright traumatized by their family, but it's up to us to decide how their behavior will impact us forever. I'm not saying it's easy, but we decide how much baggage we want to carry around."

Josie, our part-time helper, steps into the bathroom. "Sorry, Gracie, your phone has been ringing, and I was afraid it might be an emergency, so I thought I should let you know."

"Oh, thanks," I say, running over the short list of people it could be.

"Go ahead. I've got this under control, I think." She totally doesn't, but I release her hair and head toward the office, where I see I missed three calls. One is from Nina, and the other two are from a number I don't recognize, but caller ID says it's from South Carolina... where my biological family lives. There's a message, so I take a deep breath and tap on the message icon.

"Hi, Gracie, this is Holly Blevins, your... the woman... I gave birth to you. Uh, a social worker reached out to us this morning and said you requested to meet with our children. I'm afraid that won't be possible. They are all young, and we're not interested in... well... we just don't think it's a good idea. We don't know you, and we have to make sure they're not exposed to anything traumatic. We've really worked hard to turn our lives around, and meeting you will bring up a difficult past. I'm... I'm sorry, really. I'm sure you can understand that we don't want to rehash a bad time in our lives, and you have parents, so... I um... I'm sorry. Please don't reach out again. They don't know about you."

I play the message three additional times, working to understand what I hear. If she had said something like maybe later, they're too young to understand right now. Or even, let's talk first and then see if it's a good situation for the younger kids, then I would understand. Only, her message was pretty clear—I have no place in their life at all. The worst part about it is... I remember her voice, how she sounded when I was a kid.

I drop my phone in my bag and bolt. Shelby and Josie call for me, but I don't stop. I'm in my car and on my way home, blocking out every thought in my mind other than that message on repeat. How can someone create a human being and then just... forget? Not need them in their lives? Not *want* to make things right that were so, so wrong? I don't remember stoplights or turns, only the words she chose echoing in my mind. I pull into John and May's drive, not even realizing it's where I'd end up until I see my horses in the pasture. I need to ride, need to feel grounded with my horses, and figure out how to get over this massive bump in the road.

I had tried not to expect rejection. I truly had, but no scenario in my mind had been as brutal as what I received. I wasn't just ignored but told I was not needed. By my mother.

Hot tears stream over my cheeks as I slam my door and run to the stable. May is nowhere to be found, so I waste no time grabbing a saddle and bridle, then rush to the first horse that wants anything to do with me. It's Spice, who seems to pick up on my desperation, and she nuzzles me with her soft, sweet nose.

"Hey girl, wanna go for a ride?" She obliges and stands still while I get her ready, then I'm gone. I let her run at will, taking me wherever she wants to run while the wind tears at my face and clothes. It's freeing, but those memories chase me anyway.

I remember it all, too. The social workers thought I would forget most of what happened since I was only five, but that's plenty old enough to remember calling for your mother, who won't even turn around and look at you. It's old enough to remember the desk officer giving you sugar cookies with purple and green sprinkles, juice, and half a turkey sandwich she didn't eat for lunch. It smelled like burned coffee, and the steel table in the interrogation room was cold. I was scared, but the officer was kind and gentle.

I squeeze my eyes shut and try to block out those memories. They don't matter, right? That's what my mother essentially said. It's all in the past, and it's better not to bring it up again.

Spice pounds away and takes us across the pasture swiftly, then she comes to a slow walk, winded and tired. I let her relax and enjoy the solitude. Facing Nina and Paul will be impossible after this, the ultimate rejection, but I know I'll have to. Nina will say she told me so, and it burns me up that I didn't just listen to her. She's always had my best interest at heart, and she's never steered me wrong. Paul, on the other hand, is new and exciting but scary at the same time, but I don't think he intentionally suggested reaching out to hurt me. That would be silly to think, but I can't help that a small bit of me is angry with him. I never would have moved forward with such an idea if he hadn't made it seem like a great idea.

I sigh and turn around. "Come on, Spice, time to figure out what to do next."

A few steps into our return, something spooks Spice, and she launches from beneath me. I'm not expecting it, so I fall all wrong. My foot gets caught in the stirrup, so she drags me a good twenty feet before she shifts, freeing my foot. My horse disappears over the hillside while I lay facing the clouds in severe pain. My foot hurts, my side is splitting, and I know I've got a few cuts from being dragged, but it definitely could be worse.

I roll on my side and sit up, then take a few breaths before trying to stand. My ankle gives out, and shooting pain stabs my knee. I raise my hand and peer into the distance. Yep, the house is way too far away for me to crawl through a field, so I scramble in my pocket and hope I didn't lose my phone in the process.

I call May first, hoping not to distract John, but she doesn't answer. I have no other options, so I dial John.

"Hey, Gracie, what's up?" he asks, but it's clear he's incredibly busy.

"Um, I'm really sorry to bother you, but I need your help. I'm across the pasture, and my horse threw me and ran off."

"What?" he asks, and his chair screeches. "Are you alright?"

"I hurt my ankle and my knee. And my hip. And I'm kinda cut up, but I think I'm alright otherwise. I'm in the south pasture, and it's a bit far to crawl."

"No, don't do that. I'll come out with the truck. Hang tight."

He hangs up and I sit on one of the logs we'd found earlier in the week. John is already on the move, so I wait patiently while my entire body swells. Talk about adding insult to injury. I did it the other way around, injuring myself after the world's worst insult. I know a hospital visit is in my future, but with crummy insurance, all I can think about is how everything is going up in flames.

John crosses the fields quickly with Frisco, May's dog, in the passenger seat. Once close, he stops and slides out.

"Did you hit your head or anything?" he asks.

"No, just got dragged a bit and banged up." I try to hobble, but John won't have it.

"Wait, you might injure yourself more. Can I carry you?" he asks, motioning to pick me up. I nod, and he scoops me up and delicately places me in the passenger seat. Frisco scoots over, then gets to work quickly, cleaning my face with his puppy kisses. He's supposed to be a guard dog, but the only thing he has guarded since I've met him is his food bowl.

"I found Spice on my way to the truck and put her in the stable. I messaged May. She'll take care of her."

I sigh with relief. "Thank you."

"I'll drive you to the hospital. Should I call anyone? Paul?"

"Oh, no... um... if you can just drop me off, that would be great."

"I'll wait with you. You're lucky I was home. I was about to run some errands. Why didn't you tell anyone you were going for a ride?" He doesn't mean to scold me, but he's also not wrong. I should have told them I was racing across their property, and now I feel worse than I already did.

"I'm sorry, but you really don't have to wait with me."

John glances at me and purses his lips. "It's what friends do."

I don't argue with John when he's got that scowl, never have, so instead, I just watch trees pass once he reaches the road and we head to the hospital.

Chapter Sixteen
Paul

"Mr. Loughton, phone call at the front office."

No one ever calls me at the school unless there is an emergency, so after ensuring that my aid can control the class, I hurry to the front office to see what the announcement is about. The receptionist offers a curt smile and hands me the phone.

"Hello?" I ask, working to stave off the panic.

"Hey, it's John. Everything is fine, but I had to bring Gracie to the hospital. She took a dive off of her horse and—"

"Wait, what? She's supposed to be at work," I say, panicking despite him telling me everything is fine.

"Well, something happened at work. She showed up at my house, went for a ride, fell, and that's all I know. She didn't want me to bother anyone, but I have a meeting in an hour, and I thought you'd want to be here."

"Uh, yeah," I say, checking my watch. "I'll have to arrange for someone to watch my classes, but I can be there. Thanks, John."

It takes me a little longer to get out of school than I had hoped, but the hospital isn't far away, so I'm only a few minutes later than I promised. John gives me another quick rundown of what happened before heading back home to take his meeting. I'm not sure how Gracie will react to finding me in the waiting room, but I'm here, and I'm not going anywhere until I can see for myself that she's fine.

My pacing annoys people, so I take a seat and try to read an outdated article in a boring golf magazine to pass the time. Finally, two hours later, Gracie walks out of the double doors like nothing happened at all. She's got a stack of paperwork and some cuts on her face, but otherwise, she doesn't seem too much worse for the wear. I rush to her, surprising her.

"Paul, what are you doing here?"

"John had an appointment, so he called me. Gracie, what happened?"

She presses her palm on my chest and smiles. "I'm fine, I promise. I'm sore, but miraculously, nothing is broken or sprained. I've got some nasty cuts and bruises, but otherwise, I'm just achy."

"Gracie—"

"I'm *fine.*"

I give in and wipe a smudge of dirt from her cheek. "You better be. You told me you know how to fall, doofus."

She snickers and takes my hand as we head to the parking lot. "Well, I do, but I wasn't expecting Spice to spook and try to turn herself inside out."

"I thought we were meeting at the library after work?"

"We were, but I got some crummy news and needed to go for a ride to clear my mind."

She lets me open my Jeep door for her and help her climb in despite claiming she was fine. Once we are on the road, I ask where she wants to go.

"May said she would take care of the horses tonight, so home, please. I just need to rest and think."

"Can I know what happened?" I ask, pushing a little since she hasn't readily handed over the information. Rather than tell me, she pulls out her phone and taps around before putting it on speakerphone. I listen to the message, entirely flabbergasted. I can see why she got so upset, and I fight the urge to call her biological parents and give them a piece of my mind.

"I'm sorry, Gracie. I shouldn't have even suggested it. This is all my fault."

She scoffs and runs her hands through her long, wavy hair. "It's not even close to your fault. I had a lot of time to think while I was in the hospital waiting for X-rays and everything else. It's fine. They weren't good parents back then, and I can just wait a few years and see if the older kids want to meet. I don't have to do what she says once they are older."

"That's true."

"But I'm not sure of that either. I'll feel it out when the time comes. For now, I'm going to focus on what I do have. I haven't told Nina yet, but I think I'm okay. It sucked, I took a ride, almost broke myself, and now I'm sort of over it. It's not worth the stress anymore."

She's lying, and if she thinks I don't know that, then she doesn't know me at all. Maybe we didn't always see eye to eye, but I know her well enough to know when she's faking. And this whole laid-back, take-it-as-it-comes attitude is *not* how Gracie operates.

I pull into her driveway and turn off my truck. We still have to rebuild the barn, but that work will begin this weekend. For now, all I'm worried about is the woman sitting beside me, pretending everything is fine when her world is crushing her. It sucks that she still doesn't trust me enough to show me those raw and cutting parts, but I suppose I haven't really earned that place yet. This is still new, but I want it to work.

"Gracie, you don't have to pretend that it's all okay if it's not. I can't imagine—"

"No," she snaps. "You can't imagine how it feels, so if I say it's fine, then let it go." I ignore her snappy attitude and try to be supportive.

"I'm only saying that I'm here for you. If you say everything is okay, then fine, but if it isn't, then I'm here to listen and support you."

"Can you just stop? I *don't* want to talk about it."

I can't help what comes out next. It's not fair, but I can't stop the jealousy that rages through me. "Except you'll tell Nina all about it, and then I'll end up getting chewed out for it. I'm supposed to be your boyfriend now, or am I mistaken?"

"She's my best friend! She's *always* been there for me. Of course, it's easier to tell her everything."

"Yeah, but—"

"We have been trying this out for literal days, Paul. When you've been my boyfriend long enough to have a say in what I do, I'll let you know."

Well... "That's not fair, and you know I'm not trying to tell you what to do. I asked you if you needed me and reminded you that I'm here for you."

"Then you promptly got jealous and fussed about me talking to Nina instead of you. Did it ever occur to you that I'm embarrassed? That finding out they really, truly don't want any part of me makes me feel like a useless pile of trash?"

"Of *course* it did! Of course, I'm thinking of how this makes you feel. It's literally the only reason I'm still sitting in my truck arguing with you. I *do* care about how it impacts you, but if you shut me out, then how am I supposed to feel?"

"Supportive doesn't mean pushy," she snaps.

"Forgive me for my concern. I won't ask again."

"Fine! Why are we even bothering to try this again?" she asks, crossing her arms. Her tone is so passive, almost like she *wants* to hurt me, so I give up. I can't show her that I care for her, can't prove it no matter what I do, so I shrug.

"I don't know. You tell me." I'm not proud of myself, but I'm also hurt, angry, and at a complete loss as to what to do for this woman. I want to understand, to be a good boyfriend for her, but she simply will not give me half an inch to do it.

"Yeah, I figured. You said you wouldn't leave, but this feels a lot like breaking up to me."

"I never said that's what I want, Gracie. We knew this would be hard, but I'm trying. I just... don't... think this is really what *you* want." And maybe that's the heart of it. Maybe it's a lot less about whether or not *I'll* always be there and more about whether she even wants me there or not. Maybe I went about it all wrong. Her having feelings for me all this time does not equate to her wanting me to be a bigger part of her life, and that hits me hard. I'm trying to be something for someone who doesn't even want me.

I stare out the windshield, so lost in thought I don't hear her speak.

"Paul," she scolds. "Did you hear me?"

I look over at her and shake my head. She's so angry, and I don't know how we got here.

She scowls again, and I miss her beautiful smile. There is nothing about this argument that can possibly end well because she's not ready. I should have listened to her when she told me she was too afraid.

"I said, I don't need you right now. I just need to go inside and think."

A huff of breath rushes from my lips. For someone who is scared to death of abandonment, she doesn't pay much attention to the words she uses against others. And for a second, I think... fine, I don't need this in my life. This is how it's always been and how it's always going to be. I can't do this for my whole life.

"Fine. Goodnight, Gracie."

I know I'm in for it when she glares at me the way she used to, throws her seatbelt off, shoves the door open, and slams it behind her. I groan and drop my head onto the steering wheel, accidentally smashing the horn as I do. I jerk backward and utter a few curse words, but I'm still frustrated. I never expected this to be easy, but I had at least assumed she wouldn't treat me second class to my sister.

I can't drive, not like this, so I stare at my hands in my lap. I'm equal parts angry and hurt, but I know that I don't want things to end like this. I don't want them to end at all because for my whole life this woman has been there. She's seen me accomplish things, seen me fail, cheered at my baseball games, and fought beside me in the great neighborhood water balloon fight of seven years ago. She *knows* me, and I know her.

I'm startled when she knocks on the window beside me. I jump a little, but when I focus, I see tears streaming down her face, so much pain in her eyes, and an expression that begs me to open the door.

I yank my seatbelt off and she moves back so I can throw my door open. One step, and she's in my arms, sobbing.

"I'm so sorry. I don't know why I said all of those things." She's got a tight hold on my shirtfront and pulling still more with each breath. Her sobs are so hard she's practically hiccupping to breathe, and her whole body is tense. So I pick her up. I lift her into my arms and carry her to her front door, where I only let her go for long enough to pry the key from her hand and unlock the door, then I've got her again.

I drop the keys on her side table and sit on the sofa with her, holding her while she cries out everything that's holding her down. It's a lot, and she's like a small child this way, but I think maybe that's okay. Maybe Gracie, the child, needs to let it all go before Gracie, the adult, can move on. And if it takes all night, then I will sit here all night holding her, hugging her.

"I'm sorry, Paul."

"I know. So am I. We got carried away, but we're talking now."

She nods against my shoulder and continues with bouts of tears that break my heart. I question whether I should call Nina, but decide that she'll tell me if that's what she wants. We sit for a while until she shifts and sits snuggled up against me.

"I said I didn't need you, and instant regret made me so sick. That's how I feel all the time, and I never want to make you feel that way. I do need you, but it scared me how much I needed you tonight. I lied about it not hurting, and being called out on it scared me too."

"You deserve better than what she did to you, but her actions have zero reflection on you. You have to know that. You have to know that this is her problem and not yours. It isn't *because* of you, but because of her."

"It's hard to believe that when it's your mother," she says, leaning her head on my chest.

"But she isn't your mother. Your mother loves you as you are. We all do."

She says nothing more but pushes up to kiss my cheek before settling in again. She's exhausted, and I have nowhere else I want to be, so I settle back and let her use me as a pillow. Her soft breaths become steady and her body soon relaxes, so I lean my head back and try to get a little rest. Emotionally, she's spent, and I'm not far behind, but I know we're not out of the hard part yet.

Chapter Seventeen

Gracie

SOMETIME AFTER MIDNIGHT, I wake on the sofa with a stiff neck, wrapped in Paul's arms. He hadn't left, even when he had a lot of good reasons to walk away. I said things I hadn't meant, eliciting reactions from him I knew I would get. It was like I sought them out because it was better to force the negative result—angering him into leaving—than to hope for the positive—that he meant what he said, he wouldn't leave, and this thing between us was growing into something terrifyingly real.

Thank God he hadn't put his Jeep in reverse and bolted.

Looking at him now, how quiet and peaceful he is, content to be stuck here holding me while I sleep, I can't imagine why I wouldn't dive in head first with him. Leap right into the thing I wanted for so long. Trauma sucks, but I have to find a way to stop it from ruining the best parts of my life.

But all good things have a time limit, and my ability to freely stare at the most handsome man in the world is abruptly cut short when he jerks in his sleep, and his eyes pop open. I gasp, and he focuses on me, eyes narrowed. He looks around to orient himself, then clears his throat.

"Sorry. I had a dream I was chasing Frisco around the backyard because he stole my gradebook."

"That is an oddly specific dream, but it also seems like something he would do." I roll to the side and sit while trying to tame my wild red hair.

"Don't do that. You look beautiful." Paul's groggy voice gives me chills, but I don't stop trying to manage this long mess of waves. It's always been a thick pain in the rear to control, but in my work, I don't notice him scowl at me. He grabs me around the waist and yanks me across the sofa. "I *said* you look beautiful. Kiss me."

I dodge him and squeal. "I just woke up! I haven't even brushed my teeth!"

He checks his watch. "It's midnight, geez."

"I know. I'm sorry. You have to work tomorrow, and I kept you here way too late."

"I got tomorrow off. I wasn't sure if you would need help, so when I left today, I put in for a substitute tomorrow." He settles into the sofa casually, as if taking time off from work for me is not a big deal. Well, it is to me.

"You took off for me?"

"Yeah," he drawls. "You're my girl, and you got hurt. Why wouldn't I take off to help you out?"

"I guess it's just unexpected, but I'm glad you did. Maybe I can call in tomorrow and relax. I think I need a break. Things around here have been completely crazy, and then this thing with my siblings is emotionally draining."

Paul pulls me close again and snuggles his arms around me. "I think that's a good plan. We can do something fun if you're not too sore. Or we can be lazy and sit around all day doing nothing."

"I should go help May at least. I kind of dumped a lot of work on her."

"Oh!" Paul shouts and sits straight, so fast I almost roll onto the floor. "I forgot with everything going on. I was going to tell you after work, but... Anyway, John wants to offer you a job."

"A job? First, why didn't he say so himself on the way to the hospital? And second, he knows I'm not a lawyer or aid or anything, so what on earth kind of job would he have for me?"

Paul's lip quirks up on one side, and he tilts his head. "Um, you had just been thrown by a horse, so my guess is he was more worried about that than a job offer, plus he asked me to talk to you about it. He probably wanted to give me a chance to present it to you. It's kind of a big deal, and it doesn't have anything to do with his law firm."

"Okay," I say, a bit nervous. I don't hate my job at the library, but there are certainly other jobs that might pay better and be more enjoyable than scraping boogers and jelly from the inside of books or chasing our resident duck from the lobby.

"May wants to start a therapy farm. I guess all of those animals you sent her gave her the idea, but anyway, she needs a lot of help. John said he'd pay you more than you make now, and when things get set up, he could give you a raise. If you're interested, you're supposed to talk with him about it."

"Wonder why he didn't just ask me himself?" I bite my lip, trying not to seem too eager about this dream of a job.

Paul chuckles. "They wanted to give me some bonus points with you, I guess. I don't know. I love my brother, but sometimes his ideas are ridiculous. Anyway, what do you think?"

"Points? Like brownie points?" I ask with a smirk. He nods and rolls his eyes. "Mmm, I see. Well, points earned, and I'm definitely interested. Maybe we can talk to them tomorrow, but for now, you should probably get home and get some sleep if we're going to have an awesome day of fun tomorrow."

"Nope, not going anywhere. I told you I wasn't going to leave you while you were upset, and you can't possibly feel better already, so you're stuck with me. So, movie or more sleep?"

He means it. He's not budging, but I'm so tired from the pain medication that I know I'll never make it through a movie, and trying would mean falling asleep on the sofa again. I will definitely be sore if I do that, so I nod toward the guest room.

"Sleep, but I'm going to bed. You can take the guest room, and I'll see you in the morning."

"What? What kind of idea is that? No more sofa snuggling?" He tries to pout, but he's never been any good at it, and he knows it, so he changes tactics when I roll my eyes. "Come here, beautiful." He's lowered his voice, but as alluring as it is, I'm not falling for the Paul Loughton charm.

I scrunch my nose at him and head down the hallway. Halfway down, I hear him thumping down the hall in a jog. I'm toast, I know, but there's nothing I can do about it. My bedroom is still too far away, and getting the door shut and locked is impossible with him already right behind me. He grabs me around the waist and hauls me over his shoulder before carrying me back to the living room.

"Put me down!" I squeal, but I can't bring myself to put on my stern tone. I can only giggle because his fingers dig into my sides. It's a little uncomfortable, given my bruising, but I wouldn't trade playing with Paul for anything in the world.

"I can't hear you," he teases.

"Yes, you can! Put me down!" Wrong thing to say. He puts me down on the sofa but cages me in while leaning over me with the same grin that I know spells trouble. His dirty blonde hair sticks up everywhere, which makes me smile. It isn't like we've never been playful with one another. I remember those moments now, too. For the life of me, I can't figure out why I only committed the bad things to memory, why I only saw the arguments and tension between us but blocked out all of the laughter and fun that made growing up with him, Nina, and the other Loughton brood so much fun.

They wanted me. They always had, even when we didn't always get along.

Paul's expression softens, and he brushes his thumb over my cheek, wiping away tears. "Please let these be happy tears," he whispers. I nod, and he sighs before kissing me. He allows me to shift into a seated position without breaking our kiss so I can wrap my arms around his neck and pull him tight. This was not a well-planned or executed kiss in any way, so he stumbles, and we both end up a tangle of arms and legs on the floor, which is, apparently, an invitation for him to tickle me all over again.

"I remember how much you love being tickled," he teases.

"I do not!" I screech, wiggling beneath his grip. He releases me but keeps me caged in again. I can't say that I mind, not one bit.

Staring down at me, he lets the tension take over again. My stomach flutters like a cage full of butterflies, but his intensity only increases.

"I want you to know that I see this moment. It's intentional, and I don't want to miss another moment between us ever again. It's not always easy for me to read you, but if you're patient with me, I'll be patient with you."

Tears dribble over my cheeks again, but they're so, so good. They're every memory between us flooding back into my mind like a tsunami of happiness and joy. His stupid snake ate my hamster... but he bought me a pet mouse the next day. I had still been too angry to see that he was trying.

He'd been trembling the night he apologized to me for the pool incident, and that had to mean that he cared. If it was merely an act his mother forced, then he wouldn't have been scared. My forgiveness meant something to him.

His intention for telling my crush I was crazy about him was to spark interest. He was *trying* to give me the boy I'd liked back then, but silly Paul... that crush was a rebound, my awful attempt at covering my feelings for him with feelings for some other guy. And really, that was what hurt. He'd tried to pawn me off, but he didn't know that. To him, it was an act of kindness, something to make me happy.

Everything he had ever done backfired splendidly, and I often got hurt in the process. But he had never meant for it to happen that way.

So many good memories come back to me.

Teasing Edwin about his proper attire even in high school. We fed off of each other so well that we found ourselves in a fit of giggles every time. The water balloon war years ago... Somehow, the two of us got cornered together, but Paul had a plan. With no more than six balloons between us, we ended up winning the fight. He picked me up onto his shoulders and ran around the yard, screaming that we were the champions. Then he put me down and wiped my wet hair from my face, smiled, and ran off to have fun with his guy friends. I'd been disappointed, thought it was yet another moment he bailed on, but I failed to see what was building between us all those years, all those laughs and jokes and fun times spent together.

"Are you okay?" he whispers, brushing my hair away again.

I cup his face and nod. "I think all this time, I thought special moments between us had to be a certain way to mean anything, and I missed out on the memories we were building. Our foundation is pretty strong, isn't it?"

"I think so, yeah. You know as much about me as the less-stellar Loughton siblings, for sure."

I can't help laughing at his categorization. "I might have to agree that you are the best, but you can't tell Nina. She'll never forgive me."

He chuckles but pulls me up to sit facing one another again. "About Nina, I'm not looking to be a downer or anything, but I need to apologize for what I said earlier. I had no right to compare our relationship to what you have with Nina." Guilt washes over his face, and his cheeks redden.

"Maybe not, but it's also wrong of me to run only to her when you are also important to me. Your opinion *does* matter. It's just been easier to talk to her all of these years."

"There's nothing wrong with that. She's your best friend and has been for a long time. I can't expect you to drop everything and—"

"But yes, you should. I don't mean to interrupt, but you should expect that from me. I know what relationships mean to you and your family. You don't mess around with people's hearts and minds. Dating isn't a fun, meaningless thing to you, so for you to want this with me means that you not only respect me but... you..." Holy cow, everything hits me now.

He knows, too, because he smirks. "You didn't think I would be stupid enough to get involved with my sister's best friend if I hadn't thought about a future with you, did you? Because if you did, then we have a lot of talking to do about your lack of faith in my intelligence." He's teasing, but he's also not wrong.

And he already told me as much when we went for our walk days ago. He has no intention of treating this lightly but every intention of committing to something I never thought I would have with him. He doesn't only offer it. He *wants* it.

"Gracie, the thing you don't know is that you are incredibly intimidating. I loved our childhood growing up together. It wasn't always easy, and we fussed because that's what people do sometimes, but that never meant that I didn't like you."

I chuckle and shift my weight because talking like this is scary. "I guess my feelings for you always clouded my judgment. I was working so hard to get you to see me that I didn't play the long game. I didn't focus on those times that we were building our friendship."

"And boys are kind of dumb, so it's not like I noticed these things and intentionally ignored you. Honestly, if someone had just *told* me you had feelings for me, things would have gone a lot differently."

What?

"You mean, if you had known..."

Paul laughs and practically tackles me. "There would have been a lot more of this," he says, then kisses me until I can't breathe. But it's such a sweet loss of breath that I don't want it to end. He's gentle and forceful in all the right ways, holds me like he knows our past was hard, but our future will be better, and when he murmurs my name, I hear the desperation. He's desperate to keep me, and for the first time in my entire life, I trust it.

Chapter Eighteen
Paul

"You're an absolute beast in the morning," Gracie says when she hands me a cup of coffee. I've never been a morning person. In fact, no one in my family is, but I remember when Gracie used to spend the night, she was always up and perky in the morning before Nina and the rest of us. Judging from the smell in the kitchen, she still makes the best French toast, though, so I can't be too angry she's teasing me.

"You're talking too much for eight in the morning, especially after keeping me up half the night kissing me," I tease.

"Me? I tried to go to bed, but you tackled me and dragged me back down the hall for kissing, mister." She waves a spatula at me, flinging egg batter on my shirt. "Oh, sorry."

"It's okay. I have my gym bag in my car with a change of clothes. I'll be a little wrinkled, but at least I won't have to go to my place before we visit my brother."

"I can iron them if you want. Oh, also, I messaged May, and she's free before lunch, then she's got a booked afternoon. We have to hurry."

The fact that she is not only awake and making breakfast but also has had a conversation with another person and is cheerful about it is a mystery to me. I'm still half dead, but the breakfast makes my stomach happy, at least. I mumble around a bite, and she slides the syrup closer... and the nutmeg. I swallow, and my gaze connects with hers.

"You remember," I whisper.

She shrugs and kisses my cheek, then gets back to work finishing the toast. "Nutmeg is gross, by the way. I never understood why you put it on every breakfast food. French toast, waffles, pancakes... yuck."

"You mean like your obsession with all things pumpkin spice?"

"Oh please, that's a common obsession. Everyone likes pumpkin spice."

"Not everyone. It's disgusting, especially in coffee. It's like drinking sand and sugar in weak coffee."

She lifts her spatula again. "Those are fighting words, Loughton. Take them back." Oh, now it's on. Gracie's threats are always backed with action. Never once has she made a threat and not come after me when I taunt her, so naturally, I go all in.

"I'd rather drink mud. Probably healthier, too." I swallow fast because she drops her spatula, thinks twice, and grabs it again.

"Three swats for you. Don't say I didn't warn you." She chases me into the living room, where I might stand a chance.

She's got to catch me first, and since she's on one side of the sofa and I'm on the other, I feel pretty good about my ability to dodge her angry spatula swats. I mean, I don't have a choice because I already know how bad they hurt. It won't be my first swat and the memory of stealing a brownie from her tray before they were cool flashes in my mind. I got the brownie but also cracked knuckles.

"Don't make this harder than it needs to be, Paul."

"Uh, I think I'm making it easier. You're violent, did you know that?"

"Me? *You once threw me across a ping pong table!*" she shouts. "All because you lost a bet!"

I laugh so hard I almost snort toast out of my nose. "It's your fault. You made me lose."

"I did not! I literally walked into the room."

"Yeah, well, you looked hot that day, and I was distracted."

She pauses her stalking around the sofa for a second to take in what I said. With an arched brow, she stares at me with skepticism all over her face.

"I said what I said," I admit. "I tell no lies. Your beauty caused me to lose ten bucks."

She puts her hands on her hips, her spatula sticking back like a sheathed sword. She's just about to deny my claim when her phone rings. "After I take this call, I'm coming for you."

She drops her weapon in the sink and wipes her hands on a towel before checking the screen. "Oh... it's... from South Carolina," she whispers. "I'm not so sure answering is a good idea."

I stare over her shoulder at the screen, filled with a load of feelings coursing through me, not the least of which is anger, but there's a thread of hope that inspires me to pick up the phone. "Want me to answer it? If it's good, then I'll let you decide what to do. If not, I'll tell them what I think of them."

She licks her lips, and her eyes flutter up to connect with mine. She nods. "Yeah, I trust you."

I tap to answer, ready to give someone a verbal lashing. I only need one good reason.

"Hello?" I ask, working to control my temper.

"Hi, um, is this Gracie Gallagher's phone?" The man's voice is young, maybe a teenager, so I bite my tongue and hold off on my anger a little longer.

"It is. Can I help you?"

"Maybe. Um, this is Carter Blevins, and I think... I think Gracie is my sister. I wanted to maybe try to talk to her if that's okay?"

Holy cow.

"Um, how old are you?" I ask, worried this kid might be super young, and I don't want to cause any trouble for Gracie.

"Eighteen, so it's my decision to talk to her. I want to, if she's still willing."

"Sure, hold on a second, okay?"

"Yeah." The kid is nervous judging by his tone, so I cover the speaker.

"It's your brother, Gracie. He says he's eighteen, his name is Carter, and he wants to talk to you. What do you want to do?"

The brightest smile spreads across her face and she reaches for the phone. "Hello?"

I wrap my arms around her waist from behind, doing what I can to encourage and support her while she makes this massive step. She snuggles in and listens to her brother on the other end.

"I understand. I'm not upset with any of you." Another few minutes pass, and she says, "Yes, I can meet you for lunch. Would it be okay if I bring my boyfriend, or would that be weird?" She laughs at his response. "Yeah, bring her along. I'd love to meet her. Noon works for me, and the restaurant is fine. I know where it is."

When she hangs up, she squeals.

"Good then?" I ask.

She turns in my arms and dives in for a kiss. Happy Gracie is hard to kiss because she keeps giggling and smiling, but I'm not complaining. She pulls away, then kisses me once more for good measure.

"He drove up from South Carolina this morning after getting into a spat with his parents. Evidently, he overheard our mother leaving me the message, and he forced her to tell him my name and where I lived. Did you know there are seven other Gracie Gallaghers in Virginia?"

"Nope, I just know the one," I say and kiss her nose.

Blush attacks her cheeks. "Well, he wants to meet for lunch and to talk. He brought his girlfriend, who has been urging him to reach out to me. He didn't elaborate, but we can catch up at lunch. Is that okay?"

"Okay? Gracie, I'm so happy for you. It sounds like he wants to be a part of your life."

"Yeah, it seems that way. He was happy, excited even."

"Well, of course. You, the *one and only* Gracie Gallagher I need to know, are something special. He'll see that right away, and I know he'll want you to be a part of his life."

She blushes again and grabs the spatula, so I bolt for the front door. "You better run!"

I manage to get outside without getting whacked. Once I grab my bag and head back inside, I catch a shower so we can head out to my brother's place before it gets too late. My free day fills up fast, but with Gracie, something tells me my days will always be full. She's giddy and over the moon about meeting Carter, so I say a silent prayer the kid is decent, and they will hit it off well.

Pulling into my brother's property is always a bit like pulling into a circus these days. With May, anything is possible, and since my brother has decided to take life as it comes, the antics run high, and the drama is mostly hilarious. Today is no exception. We park and sit in the truck for a moment, trying to figure out what's going on.

"What's in Frisco's mouth?" Gracie asks, squinting to get a better look.

"A toy, maybe?" I watch my brother chase the dog back and forth in the yard, screaming things the dog will never understand—like having a Malinois fur rug if he doesn't stop running in circles—while May stands on the front porch, doubled over in laughter.

"Should we help?"

Frisco lets John get close, then darts across the yard, runs in a big circle, leaps over the birdbath, and goes again. Every single time, John falls for the routine.

"Frisco, drop the broccoli!"

"Did he say broccoli?"

"I guess we know what the green thing is," I say.

Frisco cuts a hard right just as John slides over the grass like a ball player. His fingers graze Frisco's collar, but he misses.

"I... I really think we should help," Gracie says, opening the truck door.

I think the opposite because watching John chase a dog around the yard while screaming about broccoli and fur rugs is pretty hilarious. Nevertheless, I exit the truck and follow my girlfriend, who does nothing more than whistle and Frisco comes to her, drops the broccoli at her feet, and leans in for ear scratches.

May's laughter has gone from knee-slapping to full-on snorting.

"What are you laughing at? You could have made him stop!" John fusses, but his voice cracks, and he starts laughing. My brother has never been this laid back. He's no Edwin, but he's definitely changed since May walked into his life and stole his heart.

Gracie leans against me and laughs, but she's tense.

"We came to discuss a job possibility," I say, hoping to ease some of her anxiety.

"She's got the job if she wants it," John said. "If I wasn't sure before, that sealed the deal." He's panting, but Frisco is too busy getting his ear rub to care that Paul took his chewy vegetable.

"You're not going to eat that, are you?" I ask.

John scowls and ignores me in favor of questioning Gracie. "Did he give you the details?"

"Sort of. He said you're trying to start a therapy farm?" Gracie's almost trembling, so I squeeze her. It's only my brother. She knows him, and he cares about her, but it perfectly exhibits just how deep-seated her fears are when it comes to drastic change.

"Yes, I've been working with some of my clients to get the non-profit paperwork set up, and it's almost done. There's not much left to do but get things set up here according to the regulations. Since May is still overseeing the salon, she needs help. We need someone familiar with all of the animals and willing to do this with us. Are you interested?"

"I think so, yeah. I'd need to give notice to the library, but yeah. This... kinda feels..." Gracie waves her hand a little, seeking words.

"Like a dream?" May offers.

"Yeah, a lot of that going around the past couple of weeks," Gracie says, looking up at me.

"Gross. If you're gonna kiss him, go elsewhere," John teases.

"Are you kidding? You and Edwin spare no one's sensibilities so you can deal with it." I plant a kiss smack on Gracie's lips... and Frisco freaks out. Everything after that is a blur, but by the time May convinces Frisco I had not assaulted Gracie, I know exactly how that broccoli felt.

Chapter Nineteen
Gracie

"You're going to be fine. He's going to love you and want to be a part of your life. I promise," Paul says, squeezing my shoulders as he steers me into a quiet little restaurant just outside of town. Carter and his girlfriend haven't arrived yet, judging by the empty lot, but we're fifteen minutes early, so I try not to panic.

"You don't know that. He might spend five minutes with me, think I'm annoying, and never want to see me again." I whine and try to turn around, but he won't let me."

"I mean, I think you're annoying, and I still love you and want to spend time with you. Give him a chance." His grip tightens slightly, then he clears his throat and opens the door for me.

Inside, we have our choice of seats, so I head toward a small table out of the way where four people can sit and chat. There's a big window behind the table, so I feel a lot less cornered. Paul pulls out a chair for me, then sits beside me, leaning in to whisper in my ear.

"I know you heard what I said a minute ago, but please don't let it stress you out." He kisses my cheek and grabs a menu, but I can't stop thinking about what he meant. Nothing he said seemed out of the ordinary, so I shrug it off as him merely trying to keep me calm before one of the biggest moments of my life.

I'm trying to decide which sandwich seems best when Paul nudges me. "I think he's here."

"How do you kn—whoa," I say when he comes into view. With his unruly auburn hair, there is no denying he's my brother. His girlfriend has his hand, and he looks as nervous as I feel. She's smiling when they approach us, bright and happy, while he looks sick to his stomach. Paul stands, urging me to join him.

"Carter and Annie?" Paul asks.

"Yes, it's nice to meet you," Annie says, accepting Paul's hand.

"I'm Paul, and this is Gracie." Paul wraps his arm around me, but I hardly hear anything he's saying.

I'm focused on the young man standing in front of me, his bright green eyes, a smattering of freckles across his nose and cheeks, and the connection between us. He's my brother, and somehow, my heart knows, even though we just met. He lets out a deep sigh and opens his arms.

"I'm a hugger, is that okay?" he asks.

"It's more than okay." Tears sting my eyes when he wraps his arms around me. I didn't know how badly my heart needed this, how much this one meeting would fill so many holes in my heart, and it's thanks to Paul that it's even happening. Carter finally releases me, and all of the worry melts away.

"Let's sit and talk," Paul says, pulling out a chair for Carter's girlfriend.

"I'm so happy this worked out," Annie says. "I've been trying to convince him to reach out for a long time, but it's been complicated."

Carter takes her hand and squeezes. "We've been dating for two years, and we plan on getting married. I wanted to invite you, but—"

"Wait, back up just a bit," I ask. "Your... our... I mean, Mrs. Blevens made it seem like none of you knew about me."

Carter grins sheepishly. "Well, she thought that was true. I found out about you when I found a baby book with pictures of you in it. Obviously, unless my parents put me in pink dresses for the fun of it, the baby wasn't me. Plus, the dates didn't match up. I was fifteen at the time, and I was honestly afraid to ask about the girl in the pictures."

Carter swallows hard and glances at Annie. She smiles and scoots closer to him. "Uh, there was another child after Carter, but she died when she was two. Carter was afraid to ask because, well, he was afraid maybe that had happened to you, too."

My throat tightens at learning I had another sibling, and she's already died.

"Yeah, Marnie died when I was six. I was too afraid to bring up something painful, but a year later, a friend of mine helped me do a records search. We hit a dead end, but we found your birth certificate under—"

A choked sob escapes my lips against my will. "You found the certificate, but it was a sealed adoption."

"Exactly," Carter whispered. "Then, when I heard Mom leaving you that message yesterday, I was determined to get answers. Annie has been pushing me to seek you since I turned eighteen, but I just kept hitting that same roadblock, and no one would help me."

"Hey, you found her now, and that's what matters. You can build a relationship if... I mean..." Annie makes eye contact with me. "Assuming you'd want that, too."

My eyes are cloudy with tears. I can't imagine not having him in my life now that we've found each other, and to know he had been trying so hard to find me filled yet another hole that Paul had already done a good job filling, too... he *wanted* me.

Paul squeezes my knee beneath the table. "I told you he'd want to stick around. Sometimes people stay, Gracie." His soft reassurance was not lost on Carter.

"Mom and Dad have a way of making people feel unworthy or like a nuisance. They aren't awful parents, but we've had to be emotional support for each other. They aren't what one would call available, and clearly, they don't want to tell us the truth."

"Do the others know?" Paul asks.

Carter shakes his head. "No, not yet. I haven't said anything because I don't know you. I didn't want to get their hopes up, you know?"

"Yeah, of course. I understand, and maybe after we get to know each other better and they are older, we can meet. I can be patient," I say.

Carter beams. He's tall, like our father. I remember that about him, and he has green eyes like our mother. He pulls his wallet out and opens it. "I have a picture if you want to see the others." He points to a girl with blonde hair around fifteen and a blonde boy about twelve. "This is Jennifer and Samuel. I'm going to tell my parents I met with you and try to encourage them to let them meet you."

I stare at the picture, finding so many physical characteristics we have in common. But as much as I want to meet them, I don't want to disrupt their lives. "I wouldn't want to cause trouble. I mean, I want to meet them, but disrupting their lives against your parents' wishes might be bad."

Carter scoffs. "Honestly, I think they would love knowing they have an older sister. I'm really looking forward to getting to know you, Gracie." Carter's tone is soft and sincere.

We spend the next two hours laughing and getting to now one another. I try not to blush like crazy whenever Paul shows me affection in front of them. I'm officially invited to their wedding, but it's still open as to when it will be. Still, knowing he wants me there and that Annie is equally as excited to get to know us fills that void even more.

"So, how long have you two been married?" Annie asks.

"Oh, we... he... we're..." I stammer, which makes Paul's slick little grin appear.

"I think what she's trying to say is that we're not married... yet," he says. My eyes go wide, but Carter and Annie laugh it off. They don't know our history, not yet, but Paul only winks at me when I give him narrowed eyes and a questioning gaze.

"We've grown up together. She's always been my sister's annoying best friend," he teases.

"Oh no, you've been my best friend's super annoying brother, but nice try," I say, pinching his arm.

"See? Annoying." Paul rolls his eyes, but I hope he knows he's going to pay for that later.

I know the time to go our separate ways is coming when Carter checks his watch. "We'll have to get back on the road soon, but I want to talk to you more. Can we come down for a weekend sometime?"

"Of course. I'm doing some repairs at my house right now, but I'd be glad to have you if you don't mind a little construction."

"Not at all." He rises reluctantly and reaches for me. After another hug, I fight back tears as I watch my brother and future sister-in-law leave the restaurant—in smiles, thankfully—and get into his car to head back to South Carolina. I don't know what will happen when his parents discover we've met or whether they will let me see the others or not, but I know Carter is in my life to stay.

"I told you he would adore you, and his girlfriend is pretty great, too." Paul's constant support got me through the first half of our meeting, and in the second half he was the comedic relief we needed while I explained what happened to me. All in all, he and Annie got us through something that could have been a lot harder, and I know my heart doesn't stand a chance.

I know I'm falling in love with Paul, and there's no way to stop it. I don't *want* to stop it, but that doesn't mean I'm not still scared.

Once in Paul's Jeep, I realize there's someone else who should know about this. "I should probably call and talk to Nina. This is big news."

"Want to stop by her office?" he asks.

"Probably should. Things have been tense between us as it is, so if you don't mind."

"Today is all about you, Gracie."

We head to Nina's office to find her stressing out over a missing order of copy paper. It doesn't seem like a big deal to me, but she's so worked up she's practically crying, so Paul offers to pick some up at the office supply store. Once he's gone, I try to dig into the heart of what's going on with my best friend. It's not like her to lose it over something so trivial.

"What's going on? Really?"

"Nothing. I'm just tired. Tons of filings are due soon. John is working overtime trying to help me after our attorney up and walked out, and I miss my bestie."

"Is there anything I can do to help?"

"Yes, keep your dress shopping appointment with me because I seriously need a break. You will be attending the wedding with Paul, I assume?" she asks. I assume so since we are dating, but I take this as a lead-in to admit what I've done.

"We haven't talked about it, but I assume so. We just got done with lunch, and I need to tell you something. Hopefully, it will cheer you up." I bite my lip as she turns from the filing cabinet with her famous *what did you do* glare. "I reached out to my biological family against your advice. It went badly at first, but then my oldest brother contacted me. He drove up from South Carolina, and I met him and his girlfriend for lunch."

Her eyebrows go higher. "And?"

"And, he's so great. We hit it off so well, and he wants to build a relationship. He's even going to try to convince his parents to let me see the younger two." I don't mention the death of one of my siblings, mostly because her work is already stressful, and I want this to be happy news only. I'll tell her later, once I'm sure she's doing okay and prepared to listen to me sob over a person I never got to meet.

"Gracie, that's..." She huffs, and I think she's angry, but she smiles. "Maybe Paul was right. Maybe I shouldn't be trying to protect you so much. I'm... I'm really happy for you. That's amazing news."

"Yeah?" I ask because I hear the words, but her facial expression says so much more.

She sighs and sits behind her desk, exhausted. "I truly am happy for you, and I want to hear every single detail about all of it. I really do. I'm just..." She sits straighter in her chair and motions for me to come closer. "I'm having second thoughts about this."

"Second thoughts about what, exactly?" *Please* don't let her say she's doubting Paul. I do not want to be in the middle of a sibling argument.

"This place, my agency. I love the work, but..." She lowers her gaze and shakes her head. "I'm just being selfish, that's all. I need to refocus because this is important. It's just that suddenly, I'm exhausted and moody all of the time. I can't keep up, but I'm going to have to."

"Nina, maybe you and Rhodes need a vacation or—"

"No, it's not possible. I have too much on a deadline but don't worry about me. Everything will be fine. I just need to remember why I started this agency, and it will keep me going."

Paul returns with the case of printer paper, so I can't press Nina anymore, but I have a good feeling my bestie is on the verge of a breakdown. It wouldn't be the first time she pushed herself too hard. Nina has always been an overachiever, constantly pushing herself to the breaking point, but she never notices until the damage is done. Sure, she was valedictorian of our class and graduated college with all kinds of bright and shiny honors, but it was at the cost of almost every relationship that meant anything to her. No man stood a chance with her, not when she had goals to reach... except Rhodes, who waited patiently on the sidelines until she took a breath, then he swooped in and swept her off her feet before she could think twice.

Paul checks his watch. "It's getting late if you want to get back over to John's to exercise the horses before dinner."

"Yeah," Nina says, waving us off. "I'll be here a while anyway. Have fun, and I'll see you for dress shopping?"

"Sure," I say and hug her goodbye.

For now, I'll let Nina do what she does, but soon, I'll need to step in and remind her that she's only human and needs a break sometimes. Surely, there are other people who can take over so she can take a short vacation. A plan takes shape in my mind, and I have the perfect idea by the time we reach John and May's farm, assuming I can get Rhodes in on the idea.

"You gonna tell me what you're thinking about over there, or do I have to guess?" Paul asks, squeezing my knee.

"Just trying to figure out how to get Nina to take a break, that's all."

"Good luck. Also, I am not riding any of those horses, so give me all the other chores, especially if they include kissing you in the stable." He winks, but I've already planned a nice, long meeting for later, so I grin and go back to working out the kinks in my plan to get Nina and Rhodes to go on a vacation for the first time in... well... ever.

Chapter Twenty
Paul

"I CAN'T BELIEVE TWO of my big brothers are married," Nina says, her eyes still red from the ceremony.

"You and me both. I never thought those two would catch up to us," Rhodes teases, his arm wrapped around my sister's shoulders. She's been significantly more emotional, and he seems at as much of a loss for ways to comfort her as we are.

Shockingly, Calliope got through the entire ceremony without incident, but the same cannot be said for the reception. Three people are trying to get her veil down from the roof of the church, but at least no injuries were sustained when she took it off and it went flying.

"We scored pretty nice sisters-in-law, at least," I say, hoping it's the right thing so she doesn't burst into tears again. I have no clue what is up with my sister, but for a week, she's been weepy and tired. Gracie is convinced she needs a break, just a nice vacation to recover and relax, but I know Nina. It's more than that. I'm not saying a vacation wouldn't help, but it's not the root issue.

"Mmm, that's true. How are things with you and Gracie?"

"Is that your sly way of asking if we'll ever get married?" I ask, eyebrow raised.

She glares at me. "No, but I wouldn't be opposed."

"We've barely been dating two weeks, Nina," I say, but I already know. Gracie and I have been dancing around feelings for way, way too long to *not* know what comes next. It doesn't have to be rushed, not like Edwin and John, the men who leaped right to the alter the second their forever love fell into their laps. They knew they wanted and went headlong into it, but I want to savor every second of watching Gracie Gallagher fall in love with me. And to be honest, I'm really enjoying the fall myself. I know where we'll end, so there's no reason not to go slow and reap the benefits of that confidence.

"Maybe, but so far, it seems to be a trait among the Loughton brothers to fall in love and rush to the altar. It's romantic in so many ways, but I guess you're right, too. You and Gracie have history, and that changes things." Nina tries not to scrunch her face, but there's no use. A whole new bout of tears begins, and since I have no idea what I did wrong, I pawn my dear sister off on my mother and slip away to find Gracie. She's been chatting with May for ten minutes, and I want to steal my girlfriend back. I'm sick of attending weddings alone, and now that I have a gorgeous girlfriend, I'm not sharing her.

I slip in behind her and grab her around the waist, eliciting a squeal.

"Paul!"

I whisk her away, much to her dismay, but once I have her in my arms, she relaxes.

"I want to dance with my girlfriend. What's the crime in that?"

"None, I suppose. It feels so strange hearing you call me your girlfriend, but I think it has a nice ring to it."

Her eyes have a different light in them now, ever since she met with Carter. I can't say why she doesn't worry about abandonment or rejection from him, but I'm also not going to question it. I like to think maybe I was at least partly right that the sibling connection fills some voids people don't know they have, especially those in estranged and difficult relationships. Carter has messaged her twice in the past week, keeping her up to date with the status of his parents' denial. So far, it seems like it will be a while before she will see her other two siblings, but she's patient.

Gracie glances toward Nina, and her light fades.

"Hey, what's wrong?" I tip her chin up so I can look into her pretty eyes. She smiles, but it's forced, and she looks back toward my sister.

"I'm worried about her, that's all. You know how she is, but it seems like more this time. She desperately needs a break, but I can't convince her to take a vacation. Even Rhodes is pretty sure she's going to slam into burnout before she will agree to take a break."

"What if I told you I was working on some things, and I might know a way to get her to go on a trip?" I ask, squeezing her so she'll look at me again.

"I'm listening," I say.

"While Christian and I were working on the barn a few evenings ago, I mentioned my sister and how overworked she is. Our conversation led around to vacation spots, and he said his brother owns a vacation rental."

"Really? Where?"

I raise an eyebrow. "Ireland, his hometown near the coast. He gave me the contact information, and I looked into it."

"I've seen pictures. It's beautiful there, but I don't know how we'd ever get her to drop everything and pay for a flight and a rental in Ireland."

"Well, the thing is... I already booked both for them. They won't have a choice. The problem is, it's not until fall. We'll have the rest of spring and summer to convince them to go while also trying to keep her spirits up until then."

Gracie's smile spreads, and this one is real. "You really did that for her? I was going to do that once I figured out what to do. It must have cost you a fortune, Paul!"

"It wasn't just me. Edwin and John pitched in, too. They've noticed her stress and want to help."

"You're full of surprises, you know that? And you three are really good brothers." Her smile falters again, and she bites her lip. "I want you to know that even though I had a huge crush on you pretty much all my life, the three of you have been good brothers to me, too."

I make a face because I definitely do not see Gracie as a sister, so she swats at me.

"You know what I mean. In the past, growing up, I look back and see that I had it pretty good for a kid no one wanted."

"You were wanted, Gracie. Don't you—"

She kisses me and murmurs, "I know."

I don't argue with her. Instead, I kiss her until the song ends, then pull her away from the crowd so we can talk more. Edwin and Calliope, John and May... in one day, I earned two new sisters. They're both a little crazy, both have hearts of gold, and they make my brothers happier than I've ever seen. There is no question they both found their perfect match, but I know how that feels. I know Gracie is mine, and it's only a matter of time and patience before we're the ones standing before God, making it permanent.

We find ourselves wandering close to the pasture, away from the reception in the side yard of John and May's home. Her horses were a beautiful backdrop for some wedding photos, and now they're grazing happily. Gracie's stable is nearly complete, and soon, they'll be back on her property, which is also under repair. Most of the things she needs to be done are easy enough with a little help, and my brothers offered to pitch in.

"I'm happy for them. May and Calliope are so sweet, and I think they fit right in," she says. "I love that I feel like I've known them forever already, too."

"They sort of weaseled their way in, didn't they?" I ask with a chuckle. She smiles and leans against the fence.

"How are things at the library?" I ask because when Gracie put in her notice, Shelby cried.

"Shelby is actually taking over the regional director position. We had no idea it was open, but she seems excited about it. Honestly, the next week can't go by fast enough. I'm so excited to start helping May get this place in order and ready for kids to come explore."

"May's ideas are pretty stellar," I admit.

"Things are really starting to fall into place," Gracie says, turning to face me. "I think it all started with that kiss in the parking lot, so I should admit that I don't regret it. I never did, really."

"You shouldn't. I don't because it got us here. It was the wake-up call I needed to realize the woman I've always wanted was right in front of me, waiting patiently—wait, what am I saying? You? Patient?"

Gracie gasps and swats me again. "You're not exactly Mr. Patient either."

I dodge her swat and pull her closer. "Have I mentioned you look gorgeous? This dress is killing me, just so you know."

"It's your favorite color," she teases, leaning closer so I'll kiss her.

"Mmm, like your eyes. Beautiful," I whisper, but I don't kiss her. Instead, I say what's on my mind because it's killing me. I can't take it any longer. She completely missed my accidental statement at the restaurant before we met with Carter, and I wonder if she was simply nervous and oblivious or if she ignored it on purpose. "I have a confession to make."

She stands a bit straighter, surprised since she'd been expecting a kiss. "Okay."

I'm not proposing. I remind myself that this is *not* a proposal, that I'm merely telling Gracie how I feel, and that it's the groundwork for the future. Something that feels a little more permanent, something solid for us to work toward. I am *not* about to propose... I'm not like Edwin and John... I want to go slow, breathe, think through, and enjoy each step in this process. But dang, she's standing here in this blue dress, ginger hair blowing in the spring breeze, pale blue eyes waiting patiently for the first time in her life.

She's not panicking. I realize this at the same time I realize that I am. She's calm, patient, waiting. Three things Gracie Gallagher is most definitely not in stressful situations. So she's either not as stressed as I am, or... she knows.

I can't help that my nervous grin pops out. "You know already, don't you?"

She raises her eyebrows and matches my grin. "I know what?"

"Don't play coy with me. You know. You *did* hear me." My heart is in limbo. It's like a child waiting for a birthday party. I'm excited that she's not running away, but also terrified because she's known and said nothing.

She looks away, sheepish and shy. "I heard, but it didn't really process until halfway through lunch. I was dealing with a lot, and I've been nervous to bring it up.

I convinced myself you didn't mean it in any way other than friendly love like we've always had."

"There's nothing friendly about the way I feel about you, Gracie." I brush my fingers over her bare arms, bringing out chill bumps.

"I know that. It's still hard to let go of that last string that says I need to guard my heart. If I don't, who will?"

"I will. Let me take care of you, please."

"I'm pretty good at taking care of myself," she whispers. "I think that's part of the problem. I've had to for so long that I'm not sure how to let someone else carry part of the load. I mean, my parents, the ones who adopted me, are amazing, but it's hard to explain how it feels to be adopted and know the circumstances surrounding it, you know?"

I nod even though I can never really understand completely. "I'm sure it is hard, but I need you to know I *want* to take care of you today and tomorrow and for a lot longer than forever, Gracie. I know the wall is still there, and I'm trying to show you that I'm not here to bust it down but to help you take it apart brick by brick."

"I'm scared because I know how love can fail, but I do want this," she admits.

I inhale and prepare to pitch my thoughts, the ones that have been rolling around in my mind for days. "People go through rough times, and yes, sometimes it feels like love wavers, but I think the key thing you are missing here is how committed I am. I will not leave no matter what goes wrong because that is what real men do. They stay, Gracie. When the bills pile up, the car breaks down, the roof leaks, when marriage is hard, and we don't understand each other, and when our kids take up all of our free time, I will still stay because *that* is what real men do even when it's hard. Gracie, my commitment is before God, not only you. My faithfulness is with Him *and* you. And my confidence is through Him, *for* you."

Her audible gasp tells me this is news to her. It shouldn't be, considering she's grown up with us. She's been present for more than one lecture by our parents about love, commitment, and the importance of not toying with people's emotions. She's been going to the same church, heard the same sermons, and spent more than one Sunday dinner around our table. She knows the Loughton family does not take relationships lightly, and yet, she didn't see *herself* as a part of that.

Tears slip free, and it's like the whole world has shifted in front of her. Her gaze focuses on me, and I realize, in many ways, I *did* propose to her. I offered her a future, a solid and sure one, and now it's up to her to meet me in the middle.

Her little hands shake, so I clasp them in mine. With wide eyes, she takes in everything around her, stares at her horses for a while, then when her gaze finally meets mine again, her smile breaks. "You really mean all of that, don't you?"

"I do." I kiss her forehead and try to be patient, but my heart is pounding. "Say yes, Gracie."

She chuckles and sniffles. "Say yes to what? Was there even a question?"

I narrow my eyes because now she's just teasing me, but I like how it lightens the mood between us. "Okay, fine. If I must say it outright, then so be it. Gracie Gallagher, I know without a doubt that I want to marry you one day, but because you're the most gun-shy person I've ever met, I'm willing to wait as long as it takes for you to be ready, too."

Her lips part, but I'm not done.

"I prayed that God would bring my wife to me, that he would make it so obvious that I couldn't deny it. Then everything happened between us. It can't be a mistake, but I know you're not there yet. You're not in the same place as me, and maybe we both need more time, but that's my goal. That's where this ends for me."

Gracie palms my cheeks and kisses me. It's short but solid. "Yes."

"Yes?"

She nods. "Yes, I want to marry you, too, but no setting dates just yet. You're right. We do have some more work to do, but I feel a little stronger now than I did two weeks ago. I know that will grow, and I want to do it with you."

"Did you write this in your diary?" I tease.

"Paul Loughton, you brat!" she scolds, and I dart before I get beat to death with her little purse. I shouldn't have teased her, but judging by her laughter, I think I'm alright. Judging by the gasps and shouts coming from the other side of the property, I'm pretty sure Calliope has done something catastrophic, so I slow down, grab my future wife's hand, and run to see what kind of antics my poor brother has gotten into today.

Chapter Twenty-One

Paul

"Whew, that's the last of it, I think," Carter says, wiping his brow. He and Annie traveled up to visit for the weekend and found themselves put to work moving things from John's place back to Gracie's. The stable is officially finished, and now we're organizing the last of her supplies. I have no clue what most of the items are for, but Annie seems to know, so she directs us where to put things while Gracie goes back and forth, bringing her horses home.

Her property is gorgeous in the summer, with wildflowers still bursting in the fields, but it's hard to believe so many months have flown by. Spring came and went, and I have survived another year of teaching—little Miss Smarty Pants included. Gracie and

May have almost gotten the farm ready for the first visitors, and things seem to be leveling out.

The Blevens have even agreed to let Gracie visit her younger siblings, but only if she travels to South Carolina to do it. It was a compromise, though I wish she didn't have to see her parents to see her brother and sister. Still, I'll go with her, and Carter will be there, so there is little chance her parents will act like doofuses. In fact, I hope they might see what they have been missing and start working to repair what they had broken so well.

But she's better now. Gracie thrives, and I know a lot of that has to do with the man staring at saddles with me as if we have some clue about the difference between them.

"Do you know what this is?" Carter asks.

"Nope, but that looks like a good place for now. I'm sure Gracie will arrange it how she wants it later."

"Hey, family!" Christian and his wife, along with their baby, wander down the hill between the properties. It's hard not to like the man, so we have grown close over the past months working on the barn together, along with John and Edwin. Oddly, he and Edwin hit it off right away and spent hours talking about architecture and design—which made sense when I learned Christian is an engineer who designs bridges.

"Hey there," I say, motioning over the barn. "I never thought we'd see this day."

"Here we are," Christian says. "Now, what about that matter we discussed last week?" He nods towards his wife, who only chuckles and fixes their daughter's bow.

Carter chuckles and leans on the barn door, waiting to see what I'll say.

"I thought about it. I don't want to rush her. Things are finally settling for her, and I don't want to stir it all up with more anxiety."

"You love her," Annie says, appearing out of nowhere. The woman has a knack for that, but she's so dang sweet, I can't be annoyed. Gracie adores her and treats her like a little sister, and she's even wiggled her way into Nina's heart.

"I do. There's no question about that," I admit, trying to work to cover the blush attacking my cheeks.

"And she loves you. I can't see any reason why you shouldn't ask her to marry you," Annie adds.

"I kind of already did. We agreed we wanted to get married during the reception last spring." I didn't dare tell them that I had already been ring shopping, nor that the thing had been burning a hole in my pocket for weeks. It's not the right time, not yet. Not with so much up in the air with her younger brother and sister, the therapy farm about to open, and all of the other things that go along with life progressing. "I don't want to overwhelm her with wedding plans. She's got enough to deal with."

Annie takes Carter's hand and smiles. "What if I told you that she's just waiting for you to ask her officially?"

I drop a hooklike contraption on my toes and squeal, but I cannot be distracted from Annie's statement. "What do you mean she's waiting?"

Annie glances at Carter, who only shrugs and says, "This is totally not my lane. If you want to squeal what she told you and Nina, then it's all on you." Fibs upon fibs. He wants her to tell me, so I step closer.

"What did she say, exactly?"

"She's ready, Paul. She's known for a while that she's ready, but *she* didn't want to push *you*. I'm not saying you run off and get married today, just that she's ready for the actual, outward commitment that you're going to do this."

I spy Gracie pulling into the drive with the last horse, and my mind goes haywire. She's actually discussed this with other people. Not just other people but my *sister* and her siblings. If she's willing to tell them, then maybe she really is ready.

"Uh... I need your help," I say. "Find a way to get her cleaned up and ready for a surprise."

Annie squeals and disappears while the rest of our guests go into planning mode. I don't know what they're planning, but I need to shower and get ready for the most life-changing moment of my life. My feet cannot take me fast enough to her house, a place where I've spent so much time laughing and kissing Gracie Gallagher. I almost feel as if I live there. Wow. Soon, I might. I'll have to sell my townhouse that's closer to work, but the extra twenty minutes are of little consequence when I think about being with Gracie for the rest of my life, having kids with her, and loving her until the day I die.

I text Nina once I'm inside. She'll kill me if I fail to mention that I'm about to propose to her best friend.

She's still out of sorts, distracted, and frankly, the vacation we planned for her and her husband cannot arrive soon enough. I can only pray that it will restore my sister's sense of peace because nothing we have done these past couple of months has done anything more than make her fake smile like a clown.

I shower and put on some decent clothes. I don't want to waste time trying to get too fancy, but I know Annie needs time, too. The side door slams, and I hear footsteps heading down the hall, then a knock at the door.

"Paul, what are you doing?" Gracie asks.

"Gracie! Wait, I didn't explain it right!" Annie's voice echoes through the hall. I'm dressed, so I open the door to find my girlfriend two seconds from panic mode. This is not what I want, so I step out into the hall.

"Gracie, what's wrong?"

"Annie said you ran inside, and she's supposed to help me get ready. Is everything okay? What happened? Are you hurt?"

"What? No, I'm fine." I smack my own forehead. "Oh, no, there's no emergency or anything."

"I tried to tell her that she misunderstood, but she's fast," Annie pants. "I'll just... leave you to it." The poor girl waves over her head and exits the way she came. This is pretty par for the course for us, really. One misunderstanding after another back in the day kept us from each other, but not anymore.

I grasp Gracie's arms and kiss her cute nose. "Everything is fine. This is so perfectly like us it's ridiculous, but if you will kindly get the smell of horse off of you and meet me in the garden, that would be great."

"Uh, I'd actually like to know what's going on." She's not going to give in, not like this. They triggered her high alert, and there is absolutely no way to bring her down without the truth. I messed up. I shouldn't have gotten ahead of myself and just finished the day cleaning and organizing, then asked her tomorrow.

But tomorrow, we planned to meet the others for dinner.

I don't know why that thought triggers the next, but it does. I don't want to wait to propose to Gracie in front of Nina. Despite her being Gracie's friend, this is for Gracie alone. This is her special moment, and I want it to be *all* for her. No big proposal in front of all the people she loves. No embarrassing moment when her cheeks flame bright red, no awkward acceptance because everyone is watching. I know she'll say yes, and I want her moment to be all hers.

It doesn't need to be grand. It doesn't even need to be perfect. It just needs to be her and me and this love that's grown between us over so, so much time.

So I kneel and throw out all of my other plans. "Gracie, I had a lot of plans for this moment, but none of them seem right now. They're all for everyone else, and I want to give this only to you. Will you marry me?"

My hands shake as I offer her the ring I bought.

"Paul," she whispers and kneels with me. "Yes, I will marry you. I love you, and I want you to know that I'm not afraid of you leaving anymore. I haven't been for a while now. So... even though you have this ring for me... I want to know... will *you* marry *me?*"

"I've never wanted anything more than I want a life with you, Gracie."

Gracie's smile is my breath. It's my life. And she takes it away in one fell swoop.

"Let's go now. Just us, no one else. Let's go down to the church and see if Pastor Mark will marry us."

"Really?" My heart stops. "Like... right... right *now?*"

She nods. "Is that okay? If it's not like you planned, then I can wait. I just—"

I kiss her. I don't know why. I just know I don't want her to talk herself out of what she really wants. There is so much warmth and love in her heart, and now that I know how to tap into it, I'm not taking chances. We're still kneeling in her hallway, but it feels like a place far away, somewhere where it's just us falling even harder in love than we had ever anticipated.

She breaks the kiss and stands. "Let me shower and find a dress. We'll sneak out the back."

I grab her hand and pull her back down to my level. "I can't wait to make you Gracie Loughton."

She chuckles. "You're just excited for the honeymoon."

I can't help that my mouth falls open. "Gracie, what a naughty mind you have." Okay, it's not a lie. I cannot wait to see Gracie as a mother, but all in due time.

She giggles and disappears into the bathroom. I have a few minutes to gather what we need and to call the pastor. He's not even a little surprised, probably thanks to my brothers, and agrees to meet us at the church. Guilt washes over me. Our families might not understand, but at the same time, this is for us. It's our commitment, our wedding, and we'll do it our way regardless of what others expect.

But we do need one witness. There are a lot of people it should be, but I center on one. I call Nina and explain my position. Like our pastor, she's not even a little taken aback by this turn of events. We must be predictable, I assume, but I'm thankful that Nina agrees with me—it should be Carter. Gracie has already missed out on so much with her siblings. I want her to have this.

By the time she finishes getting ready, the arrangements are made. Carter has already slipped off to do his part, and we're on our way.

"Are you absolutely sure this is the way you want it?" I ask, giving her a chance to take it all back and go the traditional route.

"Never been more sure. Get in the truck and marry me, Paul," she demands.

I'm pretty sure I speed to the church, but we get there in one piece, and Pastor Mark is already set. He's managed to drag out some silk flowers and a few pretty bows to decorate the altar, which is a thoughtful touch I hadn't thought about.

Oh no... I don't have wedding rings. I freeze halfway toward the front of the church, almost making Gracie trip and fall.

"I don't have wedding rings. I didn't think this would happen, and I don't have wedding rings. Gracie, I'm so, so sorry." I grasp her hands and pull her tight to hug her.

"Paul, it's alright. We'll figure something out. It isn't the rings that matter, okay."

"I know, but I don't want to mess this up," I admit.

"You can't mess it up. We're together and getting married, Paul. That's perfection to me."

"Are you sure?" I ask, glancing at the waiting pastor.

"I am. We can make rings with string or paperclips for all I care."

I let out a breath, knowing she's right. A marriage is more than a wedding, more than rings and fancy things. She doesn't even want those things, and I'm blessed that her patience for me has grown infinitely since this began. Her hair tumbles over her shoulders, held back by a simple clip, and she's never been more beautiful. A flash of light distracts us.

"Carter! You're here," Gracie stumbles back, blinded by the camera flash.

"We needed a witness, and you need some amazing memories with your family. I hope it's okay." I might have forgotten the rings, but at least I remembered the important parts... I hope.

"I'm a little late, but I brought these. It was the best I could do on short notice and not knowing your finger size," Carter says, glancing at me as if to say *I've got you covered.* I breathe a sigh as he holds up two slim, silver bands.

"You are a lifesaver." I grab him and envelope him in a bear hug. Gracie wiggles between us, sandwiching herself between us. My heart hammers even harder. My family is growing, my blessings abound, and I'm pretty sure I'm following the exact plan God has for me, which is a pretty awesome feeling... then I remember something else I forgot. "Oh, a license!"

"I have that under control. Shall we?" Pastor Mark asks, grinning ear to ear. I run a hand over my face and take a breath before offering Gracie my hand, and together, we walk to the altar.

Fifteen minutes later, she's my wife.

And ten minutes after that, our whole family knows, and there's a party in the making at John and May's house. Thankfully, no one is upset that we eloped on a whim, but we're grateful for the party. We're grateful that so many people love us, but mostly... we're grateful May fell in love with a pony named Popcorn, sparking a landslide of events that started with a kiss in a parking lot and ended with a love story to tell our children about.

"I love you," Gracie whispers as we enter the massive, short-notice party our family has pulled together.

"I love you, too, Gracie Loughton. I think maybe I've known that for most of my life."

"I have." Gracie's smile is wide and brightens her entire face. "Let's go party."

Inside, my parents rush over to kiss our cheeks, followed by Gracie's. It's official. My parents can relax, having married off all four kids to incredible spouses.

Except... Nina looks like she might hurl at the sight of us.

"Nina, what—"

My sister turns to her left and purges into the kitchen sink. Everyone gasps except Rhodes, who grabs a towel and rubs my sister's back until she can breathe again. She wipes her face and takes a sip of her water, her face red and slick with sweat. She brushes her hair from her face and stands straight.

"Honey, are you alright? Are you sick?" Mom checks my sister's forehead as we all watch on, waiting to see what caused Nina to purge everything in front of the entire family.

Nina smiles—this time, it's real—and takes Mom's hand. "I'm fine, Mom. Really." Nina clears her throat and glances at Rhodes, who shrugs.

"Only if you're ready," he whispers, earning a nod from Nina.

"Uh, so, we have a small problem with going to Ireland in the fall. The thing is, we won't be able to fly," Nina says.

"What? Why?" Gracie asks, her hand tensing in mine.

Nina smiles and looks up at her husband once more. "Turns out, the reason I've been so exhausted is because I'm pregnant. We've known for a while, but we wanted to be sure things were going well before we told everyone."

"What?" Mom shrieks, then starts crying. "My baby, oh, Nina." Mom wraps her arms around my sister and hugs her tight, grasping for Rhodes at the same time. He embraces them both while Gracie pulls me near.

This is the next phase of our lives—kids, families, and spreading this love to another generation. I can't wait for it, and glancing at my brothers, I think they feel the same.

Epilogue
Nina

19 years later

"A<small>LRIGHT, ALRIGHT! EVERYONE QUIET</small> down for a minute!" Edwin stands on a chair to get everyone's attention. Our family has grown over the years, and it fills the little courtyard at John and May's house. Three generations chat and laugh, but our daughter is just about to pull into the drive for her graduation party with her sweet boyfriend. Rhodes and I saw it coming from miles away—after all, Kess and Kol have been best friends since kindergarten—but we still get flutters thinking about our daughter all grown up, ready for the next phase in her life.

Rhodes squeezes my hand. "Remember when we graduated?"

I chuckle. "How could I forget? You proposed to me before I left for college."

"And you turned me down."

"Yes, but I accepted the following summer."

"After I begged," he teased.

"Aunt Nina!" Sasha runs down the brick walkway with a cake in her hands. How on earth she manages to do such a thing with heels is beyond me, but my niece—Edwin's oldest—has always been graceful. She gets it from Edwin, clearly, but her looks are all Calliope.

"What is it, Sasha?" I ask, releasing Rhodes so he can finish helping the others set up.

"Morgan and Patrick are doing the thing again," she says, alluding to the new habit my twins have taken to—risking life and limb seeing who can make the highest jumps with their horses. I grumble, but John beats me to it.

"You finish up here. I'll go scare the life out of them myself," he teases.

"Thanks." I huff and take the cake from Sasha, then smile as she rushes back for more food. She's the sweetest of the kids, honestly, but I don't dare say that to my own. I already hear John screaming at my youngest kids to get their butts out of his field and put the horses up before Kess arrives, but it'll take a little more than that to get them to listen.

"Whew, I can't believe Kess is graduating already." Gracie's hand brushes over my back, and then she pulls me in for a hug. "How are you feeling about this?"

I inhale a deep, soothing breath. "Honestly?"

She nods and tilts her head to the side. "Of course."

"I actually feel better knowing Kol is going with her. I didn't like it at first, but they're getting separate apartments. I think it eases Rhodes' worry, too. London is just a whole different world."

"She's the most responsible of our kids, but I understand. Carter loved going to school there, and I'm sure he's given her tons of tips. We'll see them often, too, you know that."

Gracie's old neighbors, Christian and Cecily, moved back to Ireland, but their relationship remained strong. Often, my best friend and brother visited them, and we were offered a room in their home whenever we wanted to visit, but that's still far away from where my daughter will be studying.

"Hey, it'll be okay," Gracie says, rubbing my back. "I can't imagine what I'd do if Jamie, Gray, or Prestley decided to go to college half a world away, but I know you've done an amazing job raising Kess. She's got a good head on her shoulders."

"Speaking of, she's here," Paul says, swooping in to give his wife a kiss on the cheek.

I wipe my sweaty palms on my dress and head over to the driveway to meet my daughter, freshly graduated from high school, ready to embark on adventures of her own. Our family has certainly prepared her for many. Calliope has always kept us on our toes, May has brought sweetness to every family gathering, and Gracie has been my best friend forever. Our kids are all close, and there have been so, so many fond memories of holidays, vacations, and more antics than we can count.

Kol parks and walks around to let my daughter out of the car. He's a handsome young man, polite and courteous, and even asked permission before asking Kess on their first date. His family has attended our church for many years, so I *know* he will always watch out for my daughter. Still, my eyes sting with tears.

Kess crosses the grass as the family cheers for her, but she walks right to me and wraps her arms around me. "I love you, Mom," she whispers. I clutch my daughter close to me, savoring every second that I have with her before she leaves.

"I love you, too, Kess."

Once she releases me, she makes her rounds with the rest of the family, and I notice Kol and Rhodes chatting off to the side of the driveway. Kol looks positively sick, but I can't make out anything they are discussing. I glance away to see how far my daughter has made it through the throng of family members before navigating toward the food tables to make sure everything is still presentable in the heat.

Rhodes sneaks up behind me. "Boo," he teases, then kisses my cheek.

"Stop it, you," I scold, then adjust a leaning tower of paper cups.

"I have something to tell you. Kol just asked permission to propose to Kess."

I spin around so fast that I knock the cups and plates onto the ground. "What? Are you serious?"

He grins. "I took the liberty of approving. I hope that's alright?"

I nod and press my hands over my face. My baby is growing up too fast. It seems like only yesterday I held her in my arms after a difficult pregnancy. Many times, we thought we would lose her, but she came into the world healthy and happy, a screaming bundle that kept me awake for the first year of her life. She was worth every sleepless night.

"Nina, are you alright?" Rhodes' soft whisper reaches my ears as he tugs me close.

"I'm fine," I sniffle. "I'm happy, truly. It's just all happening so fast."

Rhodes turns me around and wipes my eyes. "I know it is, baby. I blinked, and it feels like she grew into this amazing woman, just like you. She's so smart, so strong, and so much like you. I can't imagine what her life might turn out to be, but I know with a family like this, she will always have a soft place to fall when the times are hard."

I nod, knowing it's true. I swipe away tears just as Kol approaches me with a sheepish grin and pink cheeks. "Hi, um, I guess you know by now, but I wanted to ask you, too. Um, wow..." He runs a hand over his dark hair and grins wider. "I thought it was hard to ask Kess' father, but it's actually harder to ask you this, but um..."

I inhale and let it out slowly, finding myself just as nervous as this sweet young man. "Yes, Kol. Yes, you have my blessing as well."

Kol lets out a deep sigh. "Thank you, and I swear I will always take care of her, provide a good life for her, and never hurt her or lead her astray. I love your family as much as I love my own, and I'm so happy to be a permanent..." He pauses, and his face goes pale. "What if she says no?"

Panic sets in, and he begins to sweat and run his hands through his hair. "I never thought about this going the wrong way, but what if... what if she says no?"

Rhodes chuckles and grasps Kol's shoulder. "I don't think she will, but if she does, just wait a few months and try again. That's what I did."

The two wander off, Rhodes trying to calm Kol while he panics.

Before long, the party is in full swing. The food is nearly gone, and Edwin has taken Calliope inside to ice her eye after the pinata smacked her in the face. John is getting a bonfire started for roasting marshmallows, and a beautiful sunset creeps in, lighting the sky with golds, pinks, and purples. The farm is beautiful, always has been, but with the horses grazing and this beautiful sunset, I can't think of anything better.

Everyone is still laughing, milling around, chatting about plans for the summer, while I continue to watch God's glory splash across the sky.

"Mom?" My eldest daughter's soft voice distracts me, and I turn around. She and Kol both stand hand-in-hand behind me, with Rhodes close beside them.

"Kess, sweetheart, I'm so proud of you."

She smiles and glances at Kol. "I know you've been worried about me going to London, and I made a decision."

I push off the fence and take a step forward. "What do you mean?" I don't want her to stay behind for me and my silly emotions, not when there is so much adventure for her in London. She's always been so in tune with me, though, that I worry she will back out to save me from the agony of not seeing her every day.

"Kess, honey—"

"Wait." She steps forward and takes my hands. Kol's parents wander down the path toward us, watching our interaction. "I'm still going to London, but just for a year. I want the adventure, but I also want to be here with this amazing family. I've already made plans with Aunt May, and after I return from London, I'm going to get some hands-on training with her and Aunt Gracie on the farm."

"You mean... You're..."

"Continuing the family tradition. I want to follow in your footsteps and keep this therapy farm going for a long time to come. I'm happy about this, Mom, so don't go thinking I made this decision to make you happy."

I laugh and hug her. "Well, it makes me happy, too, but only if it's what you truly want."

She squeezes me and releases me, keeping ahold of my hands. But behind her, Kol is pulling a little velvet box from the pocket of his pants. His mother presses her hand over her mouth, working hard to keep her squealing inside while her husband beams. Rhodes wraps his arm around me and squeezes my shoulders, gazing at our eldest child with adoration.

"Kess?" Kol's voice shakes as he kneels. They're young, but their love has grown over eighteen years of life shared together. If ever there were two kids meant to be together, it was Kess and Kol. Kess turns around and gasps.

"Kol?" Her hands cover her mouth, and blush takes her cheeks.

"Kess, you've been my best friend since before we could talk, and I've known since I was fifteen that I'd want to marry you. I'm kind of freaking out right now, so I'm sorry I'm shaking, but... would... would you marry me?"

Kess flings herself at Kol and nearly takes him to the ground, but he recovers. "Yes! Yes, I'll marry you!"

Off to the side in the courtyard, our family cheers. I hear each of my siblings and their wives, our parents and theirs, our kids... everyone cheering and crying for my daughter, and I realize how big the world is, how love can flow from generation to generation, just as God has promised. My daughter will marry the boy she's always loved, have children, and one day watch as they grow and marry. This circle is beautiful, and as I gaze back at our big family, I find peace and happiness.

We're never alone in our sorrow or pain, never alone in our happiness and joy. We're together, and that's more special than anything else I've ever known.

About the Author

M. J. Padgett is, first and foremost, a Christian. She is also a wife and mom. Her free-spirited daughter has quite a vivid imagination, and her antics sometimes find their way into her mommy's work. She is a lover of all things chocolate, a Grimm and Dickens addict, a self-proclaimed smarty-pants, and an introvert to the core.

Writing is her true passion (after raising her daughter, of course), and she writes as often as possible. One of her favorite things about writing is creating a world where people can escape reality for a little while, maybe even walk away feeling hopeful about the real world around them. When it comes to reading, she loves a book that can make her forget where she is, no matter the genre. If she can get lost and feel like the characters are her real friends, she's a happy reader.

Also By M. J. Padgett

MJ loves to genre hop, and you can find more to read below!

Adult & New Adult Romance and Romcoms

Life in Chatswain City Series
Home Sweet Holidays Series
The Unexpected Love Series
Merry Takes Main Street
Life with the Thomas Brothers
Dating a Denver Dragon (collaboration with Latisha Sexton and Dulcie Dameron)

Young Adult Romance and Romcoms

The Projects of Life Trilogy
The Demolition Trilogy
I'm Pretty Sure About That Series
The Secret Author Series
100 Grand

Adult & New Adult Fantasy

Archives of the Ancient Kingdoms Series

The House of Aurum Trilogy
The McConnor & Cunningham Clock Company Series
Land of Wind and Salt

Young Adult Fantasy
Wardens of the Raven Court Series
The Immortal Grimm Brothers' Guide to Sociopathic
Princesses Series
The Wild Duology
Astryn and the Golden Goose
Love and Aliens Duology

Young Adult Sci-Fi
Journey Down Duology

Young Adult Romantic Mystery
Mattie Bender is a Cereal Killer

Milton Keynes UK
Ingram Content Group UK Ltd.
UKHW012007131223
434291UK00004B/249